THE OASIS OF FEAR

By

MATTHEW NEWELL

Copyright © Matthew Newell 2018
This book is sold subject to the condition that it shall not, by way of trade or otherwise, be lent, resold, hired out, or otherwise circulated without the publisher's prior consent in any form of binding or cover other than that in which it is published and without a similar condition including this condition being imposed on the subsequent publisher.
The moral right of Matthew Newell has been asserted.
ISBN: 9781977038722

DEDICATION

*To my sons, Kyle and Reece, for always making me proud.
To Andrew and Richard, my fallen friends, who will forever
be in my heart.*

*Bert

Best Wishes

M J Newell.*

ACKNOWLEDGEMENTS

Thanks to Lisa for your ever-helpful insight.

Thanks to Kerry and Matthew; without you this would not have been possible.

Lastly, thanks to Ash for your tech wizardry.

CONTENTS

1. WATER DEVIL 2
2. AUGUR II 11
3. EXILED 16
4. THE FLY IN THE OINTMENT 24
5. THE EMPTY VESSEL 31
6. RIDING THE STORM 40
7. LAST CALL 46
8. RUSSIAN ROULETTE 54
9. HARD LABOUR 62
10. THE INTRAVENOUS INTERVENTION 67
11. GRAVE DANGER 74
12. THE DAISY CHAIN 85
13. UP THE CREEK WITHOUT A PADDLE 93
14. SUBARACHNOID VOID 102
15. SHADOW OF A FORMER SELF 108
16. THE ATAXIA SEA 113
17. THE CAT'S MEOW 124
18. KINDRED SPIRITS 128
19. CRY OF THE SOUL BIRDS 134
20. ELEVENTH HOUR 141
21. FADING LIGHTS 149
22. WAVE OF DREAD 157
23. THE OASIS OF FEAR 162
24. A TO B NEGATIVE 168
25. MEDICINAL PURPOSES 172
26. VESSEL INCARNATE 179
27. A REQUIEM FOR STANLEY PALMER 184
THE OASIS OF LIFE 190
   A FIEND IN NEED 190
   RESURRECTOR 204

This is a work of fiction. Names, characters, businesses, organizations, places, events and incidents either are the product of the author's imagination or are used fictitiously. Any resemblance to actual persons, living or dead, events, or locales is entirely coincidental.

Love and desire, two emotions entwined so deeply, that it is hard to distinguish between them.

Want and need, two lesser emotions that drive one's beliefs in attaining something for a purely selfish act.

Sacred and profane, the ideals separated by that which you hold dear and the thought of love.

All attest to feelings of satisfaction once gained, but not all are everlasting and some can actually damage one's hopes and dreams.

These are basic human drives that one strives to achieve.

But what if to achieve these goals, you have to take a darker road on your journey through life? What then?

Would you continue and be damned, or would you accept your fate?

1

WATER DEVIL

Goliath lay broken and discarded on the sharp, slippery rocks. All fight had extinguished from him as his tongue lolled from his mouth onto the salty, hard texture of the rough, jagged surface.

The wild of the sea gently lapped at his broken body, pulling him softly from his perch, into the sea's very depths.

Five hundred yards above on an overlooking ridge hunched a ghostly shadow. Spindly and twisted, it craned its neck to make sure the final blow was dealt, as it peered down to the forlorn creature below.

A female voice from afar alerted its keen hearing to impending danger. It knew it had to act quickly. With great focus and will, it began to metamorphosize from a humanoid twisted form with its mighty wings into the shape of the Tibetan mastiff that was sliding off the rocks below to be devoured by the sea for all eternity.

The spectral being pulled in its wings at its back and then started to slowly sprout masses of thick black fur from every pore.

Its head slowly took on the form of the canine it

was trying to mimic. Within minutes the change was complete and not a moment too soon, as the female honed around the bend and into view.

'Goliath, there you are! I've been looking all over for you,' she said.

The doppelgänger quickly getting into character, barked joyfully, wiggled its tail and then bounded over to its mistress, panting and shimmying its masses of fur.

Alcina dropped to her knees and threw open her arms to embrace all three hundred pounds of her overexcited companion. The dog, bowling her over, then proceeded to pin her to the dusty floor with its large paws and slobbered all over her, licking her face with drool. Her petite form was swamped by the hulking mass of the dog.

With fits and giggles Alcina rolled out from underneath him and pulled herself up, ruffling down her pale blue summer dress.

'Come on, you, we have much work to do in preparation for our visiting guests,' she mused, as she turned her back on the enormous dog and made her way off towards a secret meadow.

The dog made a small effort to follow her but then stopped when the woman was once again out of view, safe in the knowledge that she had returned to her duties.

Goliath stopped and sat down to crane its ears to wait for a signal from afar.

*

Across the sea from Alcina's home, a banquet of crabs and jellyfish peppered the shoreline, washed up by an inner struggle within the sea.

Sensing imminent death from the bounties of the sea, a flock of nearby seagulls descended to begin stripping the flesh of the washed up delicate morsels.

One curious seagull chick spotted a lone crab making its way back to the open sea and decided to intercept its path. Splashing down just inches away and cutting the crab off from the receding tide, it looked triumphantly to the stranded crab.

The crab stopped in its tracks and pivoted back on its legs, bringing its claws up across its face in defense. The excited young chick was unaware, however, that a hidden tendril of advancing seaweed was snaking in from the sea as it casually began to hop from foot to foot whilst readying itself to make its cold, harsh kill.

Poised and feeling hungry, the chick struck out with its beak but was overcome with alarm, when, just at that same moment, the seaweed tendril also made its move. It lashed out, making contact with the bird, wrapping itself tightly about the chick's torso.

In a flash the shrieking gull was snatched and hauled backwards to the unwelcoming shift of the tide and dragged below the surface.

The surrounding flock of seagulls took flight, frightened by the spectacle before them. But the young gull's mother who was keeping an eye on her young from not far away, stood her ground on the beach and tried to wade in to claim back her chick.

But that too, was in vain. A human arm covered in welts shot out from behind nearby rocks and seized her in its grasp.

She tried to shriek and peck in protest at her unseen attacker but her life was swiftly ended, when a ravenous mouth bit down into her plump feathery body and began to devour her alive.

The crab that had been at the centre of the commotion decided that enough was enough and so scuttled off sideways to a nearby rock pool for protection.

Brushing down his sand-stained robes, Nathaniel pushed himself up and gazed back across the sea from where he had travelled from earlier. He was angry and upset that his request to Alcina had been rebuffed.

His gaze settled onto a lonely outcrop of rocks that jutted out from the south side of her island in the far-off distance, which was surrounded on all sides by the harsh, cold sea. He tried to flex his mangled wings that sprouted from his back and winced when they failed to fully spread. He noted that there were torn, severed pieces of dead seaweed that still clung onto him. Some still wrapped so tight around him that he felt constricted in his movement.

With fresh blood dribbling down his ginger-bearded chin, he wiped at it with the back of his large, meaty hand and proceeded to pluck out some feathers that had got stuck in his teeth.

He threw the remains of the gull's carcass to the sea and began to scan the shoreline looking for a vessel to act as a makeshift instrument.

The beach spread east and west for what seemed like miles of coastline in both directions and to his rear loomed a never-ending thicket of dense trees and fauna.

Wandering the desolate beach, he turned his face from the bitter cold wind and from the sea spray that buffeted against him, and stared off to a stream that flowed inland between a dense scattering of trees.

Spotting what he was looking for, he approached a large seashell and turned it over, examining it to see if it was empty.

He scraped out clods of sand and rubbed the shell against his thigh to bring out the colour of its deep pink inner shine. Satisfied it was clean and debris free, he then turned over a fist-sized rock with his feet and bent down to pick it up.

Still holding the shell in a vice-like grip between his hand and arm, he smashed the pointed tip of the shell clean off with the rock in his other hand and then discarded it, turning back to the sea and the island in the distance. Running his thumb across the opening of the horn-like shell to make sure it wasn't too sharp, he then placed it to his mouth and pursed his lips. He blew through the conical shape in short, sharp breaths.

The noise the shell created was like that of a ship's foghorn but unheard to the human ear. He sounded it three times before tossing it also into the sea. He then sat down cross-legged on the sand and waited, as he closed his eyes to the glare of the sun.

If you will not help me, Alcina, then I know your companion will. Goliath owes me, he thought.

Hours seemed to pass as the sun fell to the horizon and the night stars began to rise up to meet it.

Nathaniel was a brute of a man with big-set broad shoulders and a rippling body stretched with large muscles. His fine stained robes clung to his heavy-set frame and gaped open across the chest.

As he sat there, he ran a hand over his bald head and felt the warmth from the dying sun dispersing from his skin as it moved behind the moon.

From the peak of the island's rock, a shadow of a

four-legged canine appeared. One that concealed magnificent wings like Nathaniel, that were folded up and out of sight, hidden beneath its matted hair. Its wings unlike Nathaniel's were not of a feathered kind, though, but more of a skeletal make-up with a thin membrane that only a bat would have.

The figure in its newly acquired form, heard the call and looked around nervously, as if it knew instinctively what to do. It padded over to a pyramid of twigs and sticks that were waiting for it on the ridge and set forth specks of fire from a large nail that extended from its paw to a nearby flint. The spark caught the brush and the flame leapt out and bellowed up into the darkening sky, catching the pyre alight.

It now knew the time was upon it to act. It turned tail and raced off out of sight to find Alcina.

Nathaniel licked his dry, salted lips and watched it disappear. If Alcina would not grant him his wish, then this old companion would.

*

Alcina was sitting inside a perfect circle of daisies in a large, green, triangle-shaped meadow made up of a thick blanket of grass.

Dotted around in clumps grew an abundance of wild daisies, that she had been harvesting earlier to make into a daisy chain. She was now splitting them individually at their stems and feeding its neighbour through to create the chain, when Goliath came skulking into view.

The canine had somehow snuck up on her and had vaulted into the meadow that was hidden from view by a thick wall of conifers that meshed into one another on all three sides, save a small wooden picket fence at its base.

Goliath began to pace around the circle of daisies with bloodlust in its mind.

Alcina, unaware of its intentions welcomed it into the circle with a smile on her face.

*

By the time Goliath had finished with Alcina, all that remained was a mound of dirt at the centre of the circle and a fully completed daisy chain laying abandoned on the ground.

Goliath finished pawing the last of the dirt over and cocked his leg to pee, then he extended his wings from his back, stretched back into humanoid form and spun violently on the spot until he ghosted into a blur.

Then the spinning figure was off, moving like a spinning top as it leapt from the island to the sea below it, leaving the flaming beacon ablaze in the night sky.

A marker for the return journey home.

Hitting the ocean, the spectral being turned into a funnel of water that rose high into the night sky, sucking up the sea as it made its way across to Nathaniel. A water devil so malevolent, that in its wake a devastation unfolded.

Any fish that were unlucky enough to be close to the surface were sucked up into its centre and were gutted alive, their bones flung far and wide.

Nathaniel watching the carnage unfold slowly, stood up and sighed a deep sigh of regret before he made his way to the stream that passed through the dead wooded area and onwards to the resting place, where the oasis of hope now lay.

THE OASIS OF FEAR

The water devil finally hit the beach at full force and the sea was quickly replaced with the sand as it picked up the crabs and jellyfish that were once stranded there and flung them back out to sea.

Far beneath the surface of the tide, the floating seaweed waited but did not strike; the force of this being was too powerful for it to even comprehend catching.

Finally sensing that it had made land and oblivious to the threat from the sea, the whirlwind being started to subside and reverted back into its ghostly shadow angel form.

Taking stock of where Nathaniel had exited earlier, it retracted its wings to its back. It then dropped onto all fours, where it took on canine form again, then ran off after him like a dog that was missing its owner, slinking off out of view to catch him up.

Eventually the dog-like form of Goliath caught Nathaniel up in a clearing and padded over to his side, panting.

Nathaniel raised a hand and stroked its ethereal hide as it sat at his feet.

'Soon, my pet. Soon. We will have in our grasp what I desire. But until then I need you to stay in the shadows. I am sorry you had to imprison your mistress, but I swear no harm will come to her. I just need her contained for a while,' he said regretfully.

Nathaniel then pointed through the clearing to the sinkhole that could be seen in the distance.

'The oasis is our first stop, but I did not summon you here to bother with Lysis, although when I command it, you may help me out. No, I need you for more pressing concerns. Concerns of the unclaimed soul that will soon be joining us back across the sea, which you have obediently helped me prepare for. We have much to do and so little time to act, though, so I need you ready, when the time comes.'

The lumbersome dog cocked its head and looked at Nathaniel quizzically.

Nathaniel tickled it behind its ears and said soothingly, 'I have another chance of life, my pet, and it is a far greater reward than what I was promised, but there is much I first need to understand from Lysis, the custodian of this oasis, before you can have your fun.'

The pair regarded each other for a while in silence as they stood at the edge of the clearing.

Finally, Nathaniel spoke once more. 'Before heading off to the home of Lysis, I need you to do something for me. My wings were badly damaged just trying to make the journey here and the only way I can restore them to their fullest is to eat winged creatures. Their essence consumed will grant me the power to fly again. It would seem that it is my burden for my betrayal; go forth and catch me whatever you can, dear friend!'

The black matted canine regarded Nathaniel coolly and with a flick of its tongue it padded back off into the wilderness obediently, leaving Nathaniel once more alone, staring at the eclipse that had now manifested on the horizon.

2

AUGUR II

Alone in his cabin, Stanley Palmer sat hunched over his laptop and was chewing down on a Biro pen.

Stan found that most tasks these days that required him to use his grey matter, were tiresome and painful. Rubbing his temples to ease the pain behind his eyes, he looked back to the screen, but the words there began to swim out of focus. He was trying to come up with a presentable and honest review to take back to Natasha, his boss, when he and his wife Petra finally got back home.

Deciding that he had enough homework for one day, Stan closed the window on the laptop screen and up popped a background image of his two daughters. Smiling at the image, he was reminded of just how grown up his girls were looking now.

Anastasia, tall and brunette like his wife but more gangly and at 20 years old, he knew she was becoming very independent every day. If only she could stop dreaming and do something with her life instead of flitting from one job to the next.

Then there was his youngest daughter, Sally, at 18 years old, shorter and with fair hair. She was the academic one who never got into trouble and had always seemed to have an old head on young shoulders. He hoped she would take to university soon. It would be a shame to waste her talents.

Stan couldn't believe that two years had passed since his accident when he had been unfortunate enough to wind up in a coma. He couldn't believe that he had come out of it relatively unscathed and was still living his dream by travelling the world and embarking on some great ventures. To be seeing his girls mature, which at one point all those years ago was almost robbed of him.

Especially on this romantic trip with Petra now, to celebrate their 20th anniversary together with all expenses paid.

It came with a downside, though, he knew. Natasha would want some serious hours back in return at work to repay the favour. But Stan knew it was worth it. She was a good friend to the family and an understanding boss. Sure, the job of a travel agent could be tough, but the rewards were worth it.

Closing the lid of the laptop, he looked around at his cabin from his comfy seat at the round wooden table in the corner of the room. The sun was streaming in from the five-foot-high window just to his right and he could see the golden hue glinting off the calm sea outside.

Scanning the room, he looked at their double bed with its blue and white striped duvet cover that was still in a heap from the previous night with hundreds of rose petals scattered all over the bed and floor.

Behind him stood the melted remnants of the ice bucket with a half-drunk bottle of cheap champagne.

Stan dipped his fingers in the still-cold water and placed his cold, wet fingers to his temples. It only brought him light relief.

Standing up, he walked barefoot across the dark blue, thick pile carpet and gazed out of the window, shielding the sun from his eyes.

Catching sight of an elderly couple walking the deck one level below, Stan thought on Petra's whereabouts. All that she had left him was a simple note to explain that she could not sleep, as her back was aching, and that she had taken a walk around the circuit of the ship.

Stan decided that he should go find her but remembered that he was still in his underpants.

Taking one final look out the window, he noticed that two decks below deck 13 that he was on, hanging off the side of the ship on a large metal arm was a lifeboat covered over in a bright orange tarpaulin. Emblazoned across it was the name of the ship in bold letters **AUGUR II.**

Stan couldn't remember where he placed the name, but he was sure it stood for foreshadowing or something.

He had researched plenty of holiday destinations and modes of transport in his long time working at the Tower travel agents, as he wanted to give the customers as much information as possible. Having hodophobia, which was a label attached to the fear of travelling, Stan in those early days found it highly ironic that he suffered terribly with it and all because of an accident that befell him when he was very young.

His choice of job offered him an insight to travelling abroad though, and gave him comfort of escape in his mind.

The customers took pity on him and often brought back postcards to adorn his office wall.

But that was then. His phobia had since been erased when he realised how precious his life was on waking up from his coma. He was amazed how something like that could change your whole perspective.

Dismissing further thoughts, Stan made his way over to the wardrobe and opened the pine doors. Inside his side of the wardrobe was his jumble of clothes. He smiled as on Petra's side they were all neatly stacked.

Picking out his knee-length khaki shorts and his green, paisley, short-sleeve shirt, he proceeded to get dressed, finally slipping on his comfortable brown leather boat shoes.

Happy he was ready to venture outside, Stan found his sunglasses and slipped them above his head. He knew the headaches were getting worse and that he had not told a soul yet. But for now, dark shades and paracetamol would have to suffice.

He picked up his cell phone and looked at the signal bar – it remained empty. *Oh well, I'm sure we will get a signal so I can make a call when we dock,* he thought, returning the phone to the dresser.

Stan took a quick glance in the mirror and picked up his key card from the lighting dock at the wall, replacing it with a gift card from his wallet, so when he finally found Petra and they returned late evening, they wouldn't come back into darkness within the cabin.

He exited the cabin and the door shut behind him

with force as he turned to walk down the long corridor.

An announcement from the captain crackled from a speaker overhead. '**Please be reminded that in five hours' time, all passengers that wish to disembark at port will need to be ready to do so. We will be in dock for approximately four hours upon arrival. Further messages to follow. Thank you.**'

Stan stowed his key card in his shorts pocket and glanced at his watch to sync the time. Then he was off to find Petra.

3

EXILED

Lysis, the larger-than-life coffin fly, sat poised, basking at the creek's edge. His three-pronged tail arched into the gentle flowing water, swishing lazily from side to side as he soaked up the last rays of light.

Brightly coloured koi carp swam past his tail, keeping a wide berth from the barbed ends, for fear of being snagged by them.

The calm and tranquil oasis teemed with activity of local wildlife that went about their daily rituals. For Lysis though, he sensed unrest in this world and an undercurrent of impending doom. Rancid decay began to rot away in Stan's mind as he got older with ill health, in this world where Lysis existed.

As he sat there, with one good eye rotating in its 360-degree arc of vision and his one bad eye fixed straight ahead staring at his surroundings, he knew a change was soon going to be thrust upon him. The eclipse signalled its arrival.

His emotions were mixed, however, as he knew although fate was assured, with it would bring upset and turmoil within what should be a time of jubilation.

But for now, all he could do was be patient.

As the six-foot fly, Lysis sat there, flexing his magnificent span of wings in and out; he was unaware that high above him, he was being observed by Nathaniel and his dog Goliath who had returned from the hunt.

Making a low, guttural whine, Goliath looked up to his master and then back to Lysis below.

'Yes, Goliath, we must go down and confront him. But beware, for Lysis is very unpredictable. I need you to stay invisible when we reach the bottom, okay?' he said reassuringly.

The oasis located at the bottom of the sinkhole was surrounded on all sides by a high, impenetrable rocky cliff face, covered in tufts of moss and housing narrow edges, on which seagulls had begun to roost.

From the west poured a mighty waterfall that cascaded down one side of the cliff face and into a large pool that branched off a river through a narrow ravine, forming a circle around its base. From there it wound around the perimeter of an island to meet back up with itself.

A narrow channel ran off to the island's centre and a cave seemed to take the water out into its darkness in the east. It was partly obscured by its own waterfall that poured down over the lip from the east.

Man and dog stood high up at the south point facing, with Lysis below, rested to the north. With luck, Nathaniel thought, they could make their descent unimpeded and unknown, masked by the crashing of the waterfalls on either side.

'It is time!' Nathaniel said finally.

With that, Goliath began once again to morph into

his vortex state. The suction he created, sucked up loose dirt and gravel as he spun wildly into a funnel. Nathaniel stepped into the centre of the vortex core and was lifted up high into the vacuum.

Then Goliath began to move slowly and silently towards the precipice, carrying Nathaniel aloft. The whirlwind drifted gracefully over the edge and pulled Nathaniel down into the depths of the oasis, where upon arrival, Nathaniel walked free from its grasp and the spiralling entity evaporated into a liquid black substance that filtered into the rush of the river, creating an oil-like cloud.

Any fish that were in its way as it moved through the current were instantly devoured.

Nathaniel admired the scenery as he traversed its lush landscape and sensed that this was all that remained of Stan's life and vitality. For away from the oasis, decomposition was taking hold.

He approached Lysis from behind warily.

Just as he was upon the coffin fly, Lysis' tail swung around violently and almost caught Nathaniel off guard.

He thrust out his hand and made contact with the tail, gripping its flailing ends in his vice-like grasp.

'You think you can sneak up on me, Nate?' Lysis asked indifferently.

Nathaniel loosened his grip on Lysis' tail and smiled.

'Not at all, old friend, I was just testing to see if you still had your wits about you, that's all.'

Lysis swung round and faced him. 'So what brings you back here and now?' he asked sternly.

'Is that any way to speak to an old friend, Lysis?'

Nathaniel said, raising his hands in submission. 'As usual, I see you like to get straight to the point! I have come to seek answers, which I feel only you can disclose.'

Lysis swung his tail over his head and aimed the tips at Nathaniel's neck, poised to strike. 'I doubt there is much you can ask me, without first knowing the answers already... old friend,' he said flatly.

Nathaniel, without faltering, moved towards the barbed tips until they were pushing into his flesh.

'I'm not here to oppose you, Lysis. I just wish to know what happened to my charge, William Last?!' he said in earnest.

Lysis retracted his tail and brought his wings round to form a shield between them. 'I am surprised you don't already know his fate, Nate. After all, once you pass through the veil of ascension, all knowledge becomes forthright.'

'Alas, my wise insect friend, I have been away some time, abandoned between here and the nether. Such information has been kept from me.'

Lysis rolled his one good eye and kept watch behind himself whilst still looking at Nathaniel with his fixed one.

'You've been in exile all this time?' he stated incredulously.

'Time really doesn't matter here, does it? But yes, as you say, I have been back a while, but enough about me, so what of Will?'

Lysis sighed deeply. 'Okay... he betrayed us, by taking bad advice from Thrombus.'

'Will would never side with her. I don't understand!' Nathaniel said bluntly.

'His mind was not his own, Nate. Thrombus played him and almost destroyed us all. But that is in the past. Will is no longer around and Thrombus has been thwarted for now, although she will never truly die. Evil will always lurk in every dark corner waiting for another chance to strike.'

'I taught him better than that, the weak-minded fool! It is a shame that he did not take my counsel, for I feel that he may have made a good impression earning his wings one day,' Nathaniel said, as he crossed his arms and gazed to the ground. Then he added, 'Shame indeed... I could have done with his help right now, never mind! That's the end of that then,' he said, as he waved his thoughts away.

'Why then were you exiled, Nate?' Lysis said openly.

'I became too attached to their ideals, Lysis, and it became soul destroying after a while. But then I heard of the forthcoming arrival and decided enough was enough. To witness this rare event that will soon be upon us, was too good an opportunity to ignore... it saddens me to think that such things are frowned upon by them,' he spat.

Lysis knew Nathaniel was referring to the powers that be who watched over a soul's inner mind state, whilst assessing whether they would make good allies against the opposing evil horde or be damned to join them.

Lysis' wings shivered and a growing dread coursed through his body. 'You better not be here to do what I think you are planning to do?' Lysis said gravely.

'You worked it out, clever Lysis,' Nathaniel said smugly. Then he added, 'Alcina too, worked it out when I approached her. She too, wouldn't offer

THE OASIS OF FEAR

assistance, so I had to confine her until this is all over and the deed is done.'

'You're insane,' Lysis exclaimed. 'So you're here to do the same to me... or worse, if I stand in your way?' he added, raising himself from the ground.

'I don't wish to fight you, Lysis, this is not your battle. Stanley Palmer will soon become a permanent fixture to your family and I don't want to get in the way of that. His state of mind is in flux and his time will soon be up. You will have enough to contend with, without concerning yourself in my affairs!'

'Stan, like me, will never let you freely take this road you are on, Nathaniel!'

'If that's how you feel, Lysis, then who am I to stop you? Where is Stan now? Are you going to warn him from this beyond? No, you are not, because if you do, then you speed up his decaying mind and that's not good for either of you. So go ahead... your move,' he said, taunting him.

Lysis reared up and charged full flight at Nathaniel, but Nathaniel was quicker.

He side-stepped the attack and grabbed Lysis' tail firmly. Pirouetting on the spot, he launched Lysis full force into the cliff wall.

'Now, Goliath!' he roared.

On demand, the force from Goliath was unleashed as he spewed forth from the murky depths of the river and coated Lysis, who lay stunned at the foot of the cliff.

Lysis struggled to recuperate but the acrid coating of the black substance held firm and hardened, keeping him rooted.

Nathaniel stormed over and grabbed Lysis' tail

again, hooking it over his shoulder, and started to drag him off toward the river.

'I'm sorry to do this, I really am, Lysis. But I long for another chance of life and no one will stand in my way,' he said as he grunted between his teeth, dragging Lysis along. 'I will not make the same mistakes that poor William did,' he said, as he pushed Lysis into the river's depths.

Lysis screamed, 'No, you are making worse mistakes!' before his head sank beneath the surface.

Commanding Goliath to hold Lysis still on the river's bed, Nathaniel strode off and picked up a large boulder. It was the size of an Atlas stone that he used to train with when he was alive. With great assertion, he hoisted the boulder up into his midriff and step by step took it to Lysis' resting place.

He looked away from Lysis' pleading eyes and dropped the boulder onto the coffin fly's right wing, pinning him down. Nathaniel then proceeded to find another boulder and did the same to the left wing.

Exhausted and weary, Nathaniel sat down on the embankment and ordered Goliath to his side.

The shape shifter again took on the hulking form of the mastiff and sat down beside him, panting as its tongue flopped out from its ravenous jowls with its sharp incisors.

Sensing some control back now, the hound had released him. Lysis thrashed about, trying to free himself, but after a while he gave up, knowing it was no use. All he could do was conserve energy to keep his mouth above water.

Nathaniel looked into the eyes of Lysis once more staring back at him from the bottom of the river and slowly mouthed the words 'I'm sorry' before he turned away and left with Goliath, the same way they had entered earlier, leaving Lysis entombed, in his watery grave.

4

THE FLY IN THE OINTMENT

Stan glanced at his watch. He had been ambling around in search of Petra for two and a half hours now. He had lost count of the amount of journeys he had taken in the elevator.

He had a made a beeline for the places that he would have thought Petra may have been. But so far, he had come up short.

He had already tried the shopping area on deck 4, but to no avail, and had instead parted with money picking up trinkets for the girls.

He had then taken the elevator up ten floors to deck 14 and had spent an age looking around the poolside, spa and marketplace. Again, he was unlucky.

The one place he didn't look for her was in the movie theatre, for he knew she would rather be out in the warmth and not stuck inside with air conditioning for hours.

His headache was raging and the sun wasn't helping matters, as he took the lift down to deck 5, to see if she was mooching around the gallery. But again, nothing.

He felt himself going slightly insane as he was

forced to think where she might be. He had eliminated deck 15 and 16, as they were for health freaks and couch potatoes with their amenities for running, gyms, disco and gaming arcades. He was pretty sure Petra wouldn't be climbing the rock wall either or taking the zipline on deck 16. Well, not at this moment, not in her condition.

So here he was now at a loss on deck 5 with just the bar-cum-casino or café to search in. With little reason to have a coffee, Stan made for the bar, avoiding all the sun-blistered tourists that hindered his path, and took to an outside table.

If I can't come to her, then maybe she will come to me, he thought, as the waiter dropped off his chilled glass of bourbon.

Sitting there people watching, Stan's attention was drawn to a black floating spot that had appeared in his peripheral vision. He removed his sunglasses and gave them a wipe, thinking a spot of dirt was on the lens.

But then he realised it was in his eye itself. Squinting and rubbing his eyes to clear his sight, he opened them again. But the dark spot had grown and began seriously hampering his vision.

Cursing to himself, he closed his eyes tight and rotated his eyeballs, but again when he opened them the spot was larger still. Then all of a sudden, a sensation came over him. It was like someone was pouring water over his brain but inside his skull. He had never felt anything like it before. He wanted to remove the top of his cranium and itch intensely at the tickly feeling it was causing.

Stan took a slug of his whiskey, thinking it might dampen the feeling, when something fluttered against his top lip. Pulling away the glass in disgust, he looked into its contents. There swimming about in the caramel-coloured liquid, was a fly.

Stan had to look twice, as it appeared the fly within was doing a backstroke from one edge of the glass to the other.

Thrusting the glass down upon the table. Stan cupped his head in his hands and knew then, he was unwell.

'I'm losing it, I'm seeing things that aren't there,' he said under his breath.

'No, you're not!' a voice replied.

Stan almost fell off his chair in fright. 'Who said that?' he said, as he looked around surprised.

'It's me, Lysis,' came the reply.

'WHO...? WHAT...?' Stan spluttered.

Gazing back down to his glass, Stan reasoned it was time he drank up and returned to his cabin for a lie down, sure the sun and alcohol were affecting his mind.

'I'm right here, my friend, do you see me?'

Stan saw now the fly was sitting on the rim of the glass and was waving at him, trying to catch his attention. He plucked the fly up between his finger and thumb and brought it in for closer inspection.

'That's right, Stan, it's me. You don't remember me, but look we don't have much time. I'm sorry to bring this on sooner than anticipated but I am in trouble. Hell, we all are, if you don't pay attention to what I have to say!' said the fly, as it swung backwards and forwards.

'Argghh!' Stan shouted and threw the fly from his

grasp. He went to stand but his legs almost buckled beneath him.

I've gotta get outta here, he thought, as he staggered to the nearest railing.

Breaking out into a fever now, Stan made his way along the railings for support and headed off to the elevator.

'Stan, wait, come back,' said the fly as it buzzed along after him. 'You need to heed this warning, you need to expect the worst, Stan, there isn't much time,' the fly said, as it landed and ran in a jerky motion along the railing after him.

'NO, no, leave me alone!' Stan shouted as he tried to put as much distance between them as possible.

A stray seagull perched further down the railing took the opportunity of the advancing fly and opened its beak. In a flash it struck out and clamped shut i's beak around the fly, thinking it had gobbled it down with one swift motion.

Stan seized the moment, darted into the foyer and saw the elevator opening up ahead just as a young couple were about to enter.

'Wait for me,' Stan garbled, as he barged in behind them and jabbed the button for floor 13 repeatedly.

The couple gave him a troubled look and turned their backs on him as the doors slid shut. Stan, giving a sigh of relief as the doors closed, looked around manically to make sure the fly had not followed him in. He slunk down towards the lift's wall, when he was sure it had not.

Feeling normality return as the elevator rose, Stan straightened himself up.

Slowly he felt himself beginning to calm, when he

spotted a daisy tattoo on the young woman's bare shoulder in front.

The dark spot shifted to the edge of his vision as he took in the intricate design.

Overlapping, elongated white petals built up the three-dimensional flower. At its middle was the raised yellow dome of the nectar with its green stem fading away as it traced the outline of her shoulder bone.

Stan was just about to remark to the woman just how lovely it was, and that it was Petra's favourite flower, when it started to shrivel up and wilt.

The petals turned pale yellow and it started to shrink in on itself.

Stan knew he was having a relapse but could not tear his eyes away.

All that now remained was an empty stem with a dark green bud at its top, but that too started to bloom and open up whilst blooming into an altogether new flower.

Ruffles of petals began to twist and contort as they took on a bleak black colouring. Eventually they stopped and flowered, revealing a dark, black rose. So startling, that Stan gasped at what he was seeing.

Then the dread overcame him, as he realised that it was a bad omen. One meant for him.

Pulling his mind back into focus and rubbing his temples, the lift doors opened behind him with a ping and Stan found himself falling out backwards into the corridor. The couple tutted to one another and pressed the close button, shutting Stan out of the lift.

The elevator had opened into a three-way split corridor that seemed to go on for miles in each direction. Knowing to turn and press on forwards and not left or right, Stan headed for his cabin as he stumbled along its narrow path.

Seeing his cabin number, 696, Stan fumbled for his key card and swiped the lock. It clunked satisfactorily and a small green light blinked.

He darted in, quickly removing the gift card in the socket and swapping it for the door card. He kicked the door shut and threw himself into a ball on the unmade bed.

He didn't know how long he lay there, but he was glad to be back alone in his room.

Time seemed to pass in a blur as Stan shielded his eyes from the world.

Swinging his legs off the bed, Stan eventually pulled off his shoes and went to the bathroom to retrieve a tin of balm he had inside the cabinet. He unscrewed the cap and pushed both index fingers into its cold waxy texture. Then scooping out equal amounts on both fingers, he massaged his temples, hoping to rid the throbbing at his temples once and for all.

Satisfied that he was done, he went to screw the cap back on and found the fly sitting on the ointment gawping at him.

'Beware of Nathaniel. He wishes to take what's dear to you,' the fly said.

Stan did not hear any more, as he fainted right there in the restroom and hit the cold tiled floor with a thump.

That was where Petra found him an hour later when she returned from deck 11, where she had been on the ocean adventure, an enclosed aquarium.

Stan was dead to the world as visions of giant flies

and dogs tormented him, along with flocks of seagulls that spiralled around and around, fading in and out, as they attacked him and tried to wrench his soul from his body.

5

THE EMPTY VESSEL

When Stan came to, he was greeted by the concerned face of the ship's chief medical officer squatting over him and an even more concerned Petra, standing behind biting her nails.

'Stan, this is Doctor Erikson. He's here to help you,' Petra said as she tore a hangnail loose with her teeth.

The doctor was dressed in navy blue trousers and sported a white short-sleeve shirt with both shoulder lapels branding his three-gold-stripe rank with his profession's insignia above.

Stan noticed that the doctor was very tall and lean, with unkempt strawberry-blonde hair. He also noticed that the doctor was obviously profoundly sweaty as he had damp marks under his armpits.

'Hi Stanley, Stan. I have given you nimodipine which I have drawn by syringe and fed to you orally. The drug should take effect within a couple of hours. Your wife Petra tells me that you sustained a brain haemorrhage a few years ago. Now it's not uncommon to have these conditions you are experiencing now, but it is unusual that these symptoms are appearing many years later,' Erikson said in a Polish accent, as he looked worriedly to Petra.

Stan rose to his feet and brushed the doctor aside as he made his way over to the seat by the round table. 'I'm fine, really,' he said, as he pulled the seat out to sit down on.

'The hell you are, Stanley Palmer!' Petra yelled over the doctor's shoulder, slamming her hands down on the nearby table.

'If I may?' the doctor said reassuringly, as he went over to join Stan.

Petra looked from Stan to the doctor as she threw her arms up in protest and went to sit on the bed.

'Your wife has told me some little details, Stan, and as she is a neurologist, I have to say she is perfectly right to be worried. I have checked her credentials online and I must say she is well respected in her field. Although you are now in my care, we both agree you have what is called and what we have concluded to be, a subarachnoid condition where the brain is suffering a form of aneurysm.'

'Look, I'm not doubting my wife's medical skills, Doc, or yours, but she is overreacting, is all. The reason I passed out was because I've been out in the sun too long and had a whiskey or two. It's nothing to be concerned about, really!' Stan said reassuringly.

'You see, Mr Erikson, I told you he would have an answer for everything,' Petra said heatedly, as she shot Stan a sideward glare.

Doctor Erikson was not one for confrontations and especially one such as a domestic dispute. 'Your husband will be fine for now, Mrs Palmer, but may I suggest that you keep me up to date with his progress please? And by the way, I believe that alcohol is not the answer.'

'Hello, I'm still here you know,' Stan said glumly.

'Sure, Doc. No problem,' Petra said as she cut Stan off.

'If you need further assistance then please contact one of our paramedics immediately. If you need familiarity then Tanya who came to your aid earlier is still on shift and is available.'

Petra then opened the door as the doctor packed his gear away into a holdall and ushered him out, for fear of Stan causing an unruly commotion.

As the doctor passed through the door's threshold he stopped and in hushed tones said, 'Seriously, Mrs Palmer. This is not good, as I'm sure you are only too aware. I suggest you stop by my office to collect some remedies when we make port.' He slipped her a small list of the remedies he had in mind. '...And at least then you will be able to make do until you finally make your destination back home. He will need to be booked into hospital for tests at your earliest convenience.'

'Thank you, Doc, I will do,' Petra said and closed the door behind him whilst grasping the list in her free hand.

Petra turned around and noticed that Stan was facing the window. 'Stan, please. I'm worried about you,' she said as she rested a palm on her belly.

Stan turned around and met her gaze. 'I'm sorry, love. But really, I'm fine. Like I said before, it's the excess of alcohol and sun... I feel tip top!'

'Promise me, Stan, that you will check in to the hospital when we get back home, won't you?' Petra said as she walked across to him.

Stan met her halfway and gave her a guilty hug. 'Sure. Of course I will. But it's not me I'm worried about... it's you.'

'Why me?' Petra said, sounding taken aback.

Stan brushed her cheek with the palm of his hand and held her chin, bringing Petra in for a kiss.

'You're the one with the condition, not me,' he said flippantly just before their lips met.

Petra regarded him for a second and then gently pushed him away.

'Oh, you mean this?' she said as she twirled for him and smoothed her belly. 'Six months pregnant with your son and two days from home. What could possibly go wrong with me?' she added with a wry smile.

'...Well you are over the age of forty now and childbirth this late in life can bring on worries of...'

Petra pulled him in close and put a finger to his lips. 'Don't you dare tell me the risks, Stanley Palmer. I have a letter from my physician allowing me to travel up to 24 weeks pregnant and that means I'm healthy, so it's good enough for me!'

Stan raised his hands in defence and smiled. 'Okay, sorry. Let's just enjoy the rest of our time here together.'

'Do you remember what you were saying when we found you earlier on the bathroom floor, Stan?' Petra said gently as she trailed away.

'No, can't remember a thing, darling,' Stan lied.

'Oh. You were repeating over and over about being wary of Nathaniel.'

'Was I? Must have been the sunstroke making me hallucinate, I guess,' Stan said, as he begun to make the bed. He had no recollection of that and to him it was a surprise.

'Uhmm,' Petra said, deep in thought, 'come on, let me help you. You're rubbish at hospital corners.'

Having made the bed to Petra's gold standard, Stan went to the wardrobe and pulled his tuxedo from his jumble of clothing. 'Looks like I'm going to have to iron this!' he said, holding it up to the light, showing the creases.

Petra, holding her daisy-patterned maternity dress up to her chest, said, 'Yup, just don't expect me to do it for you! If you were organised, then it would be ready to wear.'

Stan slung it onto the bed. 'I suppose you're right as usual. Never mind, I don't need it till tonight anyway. I'll do it when we come back on board.'

'You got a bow tie for that, Stan?" Petra asked as she studied his pile of unkempt clothes.

'Uhh, no. I didn't think to bring one. I'll make do with a regular tie I guess.'

Petra rolled her eyes.

Stan looked out of the window and saw dark clouds rolling in. 'You may want to rethink your dress,' he said, pointing out the window.

'I've got my blazer on the back of the chair if it does get colder later, though, I'm sure I will be fine,' Petra said, casting an eye at her navy-blue coat with gold embroidered lacing.

Stan picked it up to examine it. Laughing, he said, 'You won't be buttoning this up though, will you? It will be a little tight.'

He went to return it to the chair and caught a flash of silver from one of its pockets. He reached in and moments later pulled out a packet of cigarettes.

'What the hell are these doing in here?' he said in alarm.

Petra flushed red and stammered, 'I, I brought them just in case.'

'You told me that you would quit for the pregnancy, Petra? Look, I can see there are three missing in here,' he said, having flipped open the lid and calculated the total.

Petra lunged for the packet and swiped them away from him. 'It's harder than you think. Besides, I'm not chain smoking, so why the fuss?'

Stan threw her blazer onto the table in rage. 'If our child comes out with asthma or worse then it will be your fault,' he said.

'Don't patronise me, Stan, I'm a big girl. FYI, I smoked through the girls' pregnancies and they turned out just fine.'

'You did what?' Stan hollered. 'I wasn't aware of that!'

'Exactly, now you know. So back off, Stanley,' Petra said, stashing the packet under her pillow along with the list.

Stan opened the minibar and grabbed a miniature bottle of gin. He had already consumed the whiskey and decided this was the second-best option. He unscrewed the lid and downed it in one before casually casting the empty bottle to the bin.

'Twenty years of marriage and still we hide things from one another! What's become of us, Petra? I thought we were past this?' Stan said, reaching into the minibar for another bottle.

'I don't know what you're on about, Stan. I never told you about the smoking because you never asked. You, on the other hand, have bare-faced lied to me about your subarachnoia. How long have you been feeling like this, Stan?'

Stan fished out a miniature bottle of vodka, unscrewed the lid and necked that too. He remained silent.

Petra, still shaking, went to his laptop and flipped the lid showing the image of her daughters. She turned it round to face him. 'Look, our girls are fine. I'm sure that our son will be too,' she squeezed his shoulder.

'Okay, okay, I'm sorry for the outburst. You have an empty vessel that is awaiting life within you and I want it to have the best start in life. I just worry, that's all. It's like I want everything to be perfect. I have a horrible feeling that something bad is going to happen,' Stan said, looking up to Petra through saddened eyes.

Petra leant in and kissed his forehead. 'Everything will turn out fine. The fear is always worse than the outcome,' she said calmly.

Stan traced his finger around the outline of his daughters' image. 'You're right. I'm being paranoid. We've done a great job raising our girls. I just hope we can give our son just as much love as we did them.'

'We will, Stan. Don't you worry about that. The biggest fear right now is what we are going to call him?'

'I thought we had agreed. William, on account of the kind stranger that saved my life all those years ago,' Stan said.

Petra bit her bottom lip. 'I'm not so sure. When we searched his background last year and found out his name I would have agreed it was a good idea... but now we know the kind of man he was, I just don't think it acceptable.'

'He redeemed himself in my books, so... to be continued!' Stan said wistfully.

Petra smiled and turned back to the wardrobe. 'So how are you getting on with your review for Natasha anyway?' she said, as she picked out some sensible shoes to wear.

Stan, lost in thought, said, 'It's coming on. I should have it ready by the time we get back home. Say, how do you think Heparin is anyway? You heard from the girls?'

'Changing the subject, Stan? Obviously your review is not going as well as you were hoping,' Petra giggled. Then, 'I'm sure Heparin is fine, he is your cat after all. The girls are probably spoiling him rotten,' Petra said, as she settled on a pair of flats.

Stan stood up and made his way for the lavatory, when a fly came buzzing out and towards his face. He yelled in surprise and ducked his head. The fly flew on and out into the room.

Within seconds Petra had brought up one of her flat shoes and swatted the fly dead up against the wall.

'It's only a fly, babe, nothing to be scared of,' she laughed. 'Come on, let's freshen up. We will be in port soon.'

Stan wasn't so sure of it being JUST a fly. The warning still weighed heavily on his mind and it worried him.

Also the black spot wasn't quite visible in his eye anymore but he could just make out its shape in the corner of his vision.

As for the fly, it was a grave portent, he was sure, and somehow it felt familiar to him. But just like the name on the sea vessel that they travelled upon, something bad was coming.

6

RIDING THE STORM

Nathaniel stood at the shoreline and surveyed the horizon.

Goliath sat by his side swishing his tail in the sand, creating a fan-like pattern.

'I'm not swimming back through this sea again, Goliath. It damn near claimed me last time. Besides, it is home to that freaky-as-hell seaweed,' Nathaniel said, stroking Goliath's large mane of fur.

Looking out to the island in the distance, Nathaniel could barely make out the glow from the burning beacon. The wind had changed course and was blowing across the island's peak, trying to snuff out the remaining embers that clung on through the twilight hours.

Knowing that time was upon them, Nathaniel weighed up solutions to traverse the sea safely, without causing any more damage to his wings, that were still not ready yet for flight.

A cacophony of shrieks and screeches pierced the air behind him, interrupting his thoughts.

He turned around and saw that Goliath had been busy. The sound was emanating from a weave of netting that Nathaniel had fashioned into a sack earlier to hold his nourishing delights. There it lay, freshly dragged up from the forest beyond and abandoned on the beach in all its glory.

The netted sack contained a throng of jostling seagulls all flapping about and trying to peck free of their prison.

Goliath barked at him triumphantly.

'Good boy, Goliath, I had almost forgotten that I had sent you on an errand,' Nathaniel said, as he patted the dog's head. 'I fear though, that my wings would still not be restored if I ate them all now,' he said, going to retrieve the haul.

Having dragged the sack of birds up to where Goliath waited, he continued with his thought process.

He could not fly yet, that was obvious. But what if he could make a boat? He figured that would take too long and besides, it would be far too dangerous taking it out to sea knowing what lay beneath the surface.

He dreaded the seaweed that shifted in its dark currents, knowing that if the mass of tendrils had its way, he would have been sent to a watery grave earlier when he first swam to this destination of the oasis.

The journey had been necessary, but returning back to the other oasis knowing that one false move in the sea could jeopardise his whole plan filled him with utter dread.

There was very little he was afraid of, as he had faced many a foe in his battles on the plains, but this all-consuming entity of seaweed was by far the worst he had ever grappled with.

Nathaniel cursed the large expanse of sea that existed between Stanley Palmer's oasis and that of

Stan's wife, Petra.

Nathaniel always knew Stan and Petra's relationship was rocky at the best of times. But he never realised there was that much of a divide that had grown between them.

'I wish I had the strength to fly again,' Nathaniel said to Goliath, but he knew that his banishment had all but robbed him of any powers that he had once possessed. He was also aware that Goliath's powers could only give so much protection. So to ask Goliath to pick him up and carry him across the sea in his tornado form would be in vain.

They would probably only get halfway across by his reasoning before the seaweed caught them up.

A storm was approaching from the north and Nathaniel sensed a growing unease that if he was going to act then it would have to be soon. The last thing he wanted was to be cut off by high waves and stranded on the wrong oasis when the newcomers arrived.

All Nathaniel wished for was a new start at life. If only he appreciated life more when he was alive, then he could have accepted his decisions long ago. This now was his only redemption. Even if he had to make a few sacrifices along the way, he would be born anew.

He thought on Alcina. He prayed that one day she would forgive him when he finally returned a second time.

Ever so slightly opening the sack, Nathaniel reached in and plucked the nearest seagull.

Pulling one free, he closed the sack shut and bit into the shrieking seagull that struggled to get away from his tight grasp in his massive hand.

The ooze of the blood trickled down his throat and made his stomach turn, but a warm sensation began to creep up his spine as the life essence from the bird passed over and into the roots of his wings.

He tossed the carcass of the bird to the sea as an offering and approached his canine companion, who was standing in the shallows, barking at a stray tendril that had snaked out and onto the beach.

Nathaniel pulled Goliath away by the scruff of his neck, keeping a careful eye on the wandering tendril, for fear of it lashing out at him. Doing so, Nathaniel became puzzled as beneath the dog's fur he could feel a sinewy bony structure that seemed odd for a dog of Goliath's breed and bulk.

'I've never really thought about your true form before, Goliath,' Nathaniel said to the dog, as he released his grasp.

He knew that Goliath could shape shift. All domestic animals that passed over to this place could. They serve their humans in life and so to in death. But he always presumed that Goliath, loyal to Alcina as he was, would never change his form. It baffled him as to why Goliath freely changed into a vast array of shapes for him now.

Scratching his beard, he pondered on the thought.

Before Goliath became the guardian to Alcina, who in turn was a guardian angel of Petra at her oasis, the dog was in actual fact Nathaniel's wife's dog in life.

Nathaniel died many years before Goliath died and was glad the dog was a loyal companion to his grieving wife for many years after his passing.

When Goliath died, he too broke her heart.

Nathaniel's wife was still alive now though, and Nathaniel was tired of waiting for her to pass.

The thought of new life clouded his vision.

Nathaniel had returned to claim the soul of Goliath and had purposely placed the dog at Alcina's disposal, ready for when he and his wife came to collect him together, when they finally reunited. But for Nathaniel, so much time had passed and the romantic gesture had passed from his mind forever.

Feeling once more saddened for Alcina and his soon-to-be betrayal to his wife, Nathaniel settled on his decision.

'Goliath, I need you to morph into your liquid state. I need you to encapsulate me in a ball of hard casing and then we can just roll right across this infernal sea, out of reach of those infuriating tendrils of the sea,' he said triumphantly.

In tune with his master's orders, Goliath bristled his fur out and began to melt into the thick black substance, becoming a puddle on the beach.

Nathaniel, pleased at his wishes being dutifully carried out, seized up the woven sack of seagulls and stepped into the centre of the now hard-coated surface of Goliath's primordial state.

Like a closing Venus fly trap, Goliath moulded into a hard, black, spherical shape, hemming in Nathaniel with his prized catch of gulls. Then they were off, rolling from the beach and out onto the open waves, just as the bad weather materialised.

Riding the storm, the black sphere bobbed up and over the crest of the waves.

Their journey was mildly hindered as the waves buffeted and splashed all over the ball like structure, as it spun onwards to its destination. The tendrils of the seaweed tried to take it down on many occasions, but just slipped from its hard, shiny surface, to Nathaniel's delight.

With a final effort the tendrils snaked from the sea and wove into a large blanket webbing, that covered the shell, to take it down to the depths, but was met with resistance as the volume of the sphere was too great and it buoyed back to the surface.

In the end the seaweed gave up its pursuit and Nathaniel and Goliath made it across to the safety of Petra's island oasis; a reflection of her own mind and one much different to that of her husband's, it was separated by the vast expanse of sea that mirrored how far they had drifted apart in reality.

7

LAST CALL

Stan placed his laptop into his briefcase and snapped it shut, thumbing up and down on the combination until he was satisfied that the correct combination was all mixed up.

He grabbed the handle and laid it out on the table in front of him.

He picked up a long glass stirrer and lazily stirred his cappuccino whilst inhaling the strong aroma.

The vivid art deco of brightly coloured striped walls and matching furniture of the coffee shop he sat in, reminded him of a packet of kids' colouring crayons. Bright blues, reds, yellows and greens all thrown in with no thought of arrangement. Glancing around, he noticed that he was the only customer sitting inside. All the other customers seemed to be sitting outside enjoying the sights and sounds of the local life.

He had left Petra a short time ago at an open market. He got bored with haggling vendors trying to sell him something that he did not want. So he had made his excuses of needing to finish his travel review and headed for the coffee shop furthest away from the hustle and bustle of the tourist trap.

He told Petra to mind the time and to give him a call when she was ready to meet up. They had some time in port, but not enough time to go mad on a shopping spree.

Stan flicked open his mobile phone and looked at the time displayed on its tiny screen. It was exactly one hour ahead of the clock in the shop. Stan reasoned the time was right to call Natasha, as she would have finished work and would have at least gotten home by now. He figured that he should have upgraded his phone years ago, but in his mind all he wanted to do on it was make calls. He never understood the bind of too many options of apps on today's technology, that distanced people from actually interacting in person, rather than through social media.

Finding Natasha's number, he hit the call button and waited.

'Hi Stan. How's it going, hun?' Natasha answered.

The speed with which she answered the phone threw Stan off guard. 'Um, yeah, all rosy here. How's things with you?'

'I'm good thanks. Came home to find that Dustin has made us a lovely romantic meal for two, so, you know, we will have to keep this conversation short, Stan.'

Stan sensed the frustration in Natasha's voice that he was cramping her style. 'Sure, I get it, I'll be quick. I just wanted to tell you that I will have the review ready when I get back home. It's taking a little longer than I hoped. Besides, I'm not forking out on the wi-fi package on board so I can upload it to you, when it's such an extortionate price.'

'That's fine, Stan. No rush. Next time though, you're holding the fort and me and Dusty are having some quality time away!' Natasha said, purring.

Stan laughed. 'Sure thing, boss. Just make sure he takes the hearse though, as it's the only vehicle large enough to transport all your vacation clothes abroad.'

'Don't mock him, Stan. He still feels responsible for what happened with the park brake on the hearse, you know. There's not a day goes by that he doesn't bring you up in conversation.'

It was Dustin, the hearse driver that had failed to stop the hearse rolling into the barrier, that in turn threw the laden coffin it held free through the rear window and into Stan's trajectory. That in turn had put him into a coma, two years ago. The poor guy had tried to make it up to Stan ever since, but all he got for his troubles was a relationship from Natasha, who Stan believed took pity on him.

'That's not what I meant, Natasha, sorry, it's the size of your wardrobe... Look, never mind. Enjoy your evening and I'll see you soon.'

'Okay. One last thing, Stan...'

'Yeah, what's up?'

'The weather shows a storm heading your way. Look after Petra, won't you?'

'Of course I will. Always do. Besides, I'm confident the captain will keep close to shore if it does come our way.'

'That's fine then, hun. See you later.'

'No worries, see you soon,' Stan said. With that, the call ended and Stan felt somewhat worried all of a sudden.

Petra's condition, his state of mind and now a storm heading their way didn't fill him with confidence, it filled him with dreadful fear.

*

Petra passed over two dresses and a handbag to the vendor and dreamed that soon she would get her figure back and be able to fit into the smaller dresses that she was about to buy. She waved away her rights to a bag from the seller and popped the dresses into her newly acquired handbag, before making off for another stall.

Spots of rain splashed at the delicate skin around her cleavage and she looked to the skies with doubt. Dark clouds were passing by overhead and the sun dipped in and out briefly as they cloaked it in darkness one minute, only for it to appear again the next, before the following cloud passed by.

Petra decided her shopping was over, as being caught out in the rain would not do her hairstyle any favours! The last thing she wanted was for it to frizz!

She wrestled out her mobile from its resting place within her oversized bra, as her breasts had enlarged due to her pregnancy.

She held the power button down and waited for the generic logo of the phone to appear.

She had forgotten her phone was turned off. She put it down to a case of baby brain.

She ducked under the canopy of the next stall and pulled her shawl tight around her neck waiting for the phone to fully boot up.

She checked the time on her slim gold watch and saw that it was cutting into her swollen wrists.

Where the hell can Stan possibly have gone to! she

thought.

The phone, having gone through its overly long start-up sequence then sprang into life, as it buzzed urgently five times, alerting Petra to three missed calls and two notifications.

She swiped the notifications aside and focused on the missed calls instead. There were two from her eldest daughter Anastasia and one from her youngest Sally.

She was puzzled as to what could be so urgent as each call was shortly missed one after the other.

She hit call back on Anastasia's number and chewed the nail on her pinky finger.

'Mum. Thank God it's you. I didn't want to call Dad as I wouldn't know what to say, but it's urgent, Mum, you see...'

Petra, feeling impatient, cut her short. 'What is it, sweetheart? What's wrong? Is everything okay? Where's your sister? Is SHE okay?'

'Yes Mum. We are both fine. Don't worry about us. We're cool. It's Heparin, Mum! I'm scared. I don't know what to do. I don't know what to tell Dad.'

Petra brought the palm of her hand to her chest and felt the full force of her heart beating. 'Thank goodness you're both fine. You almost gave me a heart attack. You're lucky I'm not due for twelve more weeks, as I think you might have put me in labour otherwise!'

'Mum, please. Listen to me. We were worried when Heparin didn't turn up for his breakfast this morning. We gave it an hour, then we both went searching for him. Sally found him, Mum. She's really upset. She found Heparin at the side of the road. We thought he had been hit by a car. He was barely breathing but showed no sign of injuries. We scooped him up and drove up to the vets.'

Petra listened in silence.

'The veterinarian examined him, Mum. She said he has been poisoned... It's really bad, Mum. I can't make the decision. Sally is with Heparin and the vet now.'

Petra's mind reeled. She wouldn't know what to say to Stan. Heparin was the cat that she had brought Stan for his fortieth birthday, on the day he went into his coma.

'Don't worry about your dad. I will speak to him,' Petra said, although she didn't know how she would broach the subject or when would be suitable.

'Who could do such a horrible thing, Mum?' Anastasia pleaded.

'I... don't know, sweetheart. What does the vet say?'

'She recommends that we put him down, Mum. I, I don't think I could make that decision. What about Dad? He should be here to say goodbye. You know how close they are. If we leave it and wait for you to come home then Heparin might suffer for days. There's no telling if he will get better or worse!' Anastasia began to weep.

'Can you pass me over to the vet please, sweetheart? I think I should decide, don't you?' Petra said, mortified.

*

Stan had just finished scraping the froth from around his glass with the spoon and was about to pass it between his lips when his mobile chirped, signalling an incoming call.

He spun round from staring at the overhead television above the bar, showing a programme about snow leopards, and picked up his phone from the table.

'Hello, darling. You ready?'

'Yes love, I am. Where are you? I think it's about to bucket down soon and I don't want to be caught out in this weather,' Petra replied, keeping her cool.

'If you tell me where you are, then I will come find you, as I'm done here,' Stan said, as he placed the spoon in the empty glass and snatched up his brown leather briefcase.

Petra carried on talking to him as he hurried out of the café and made for the vicinity of the market. The wind was picking up and rain had begun to sleet down.

Stan felt goosebumps prickle on his arms and legs as he wove through the throng of people bustling about.

Eventually he found Petra huddling under a market stall's canopy and she had bought an oversized jumper that she was now wearing over her maternity dress.

'Right where you said you'd be,' Stan said, smiling as he threw his arms around her for an embrace.

Petra brought her head into his chest and squeezed him tight, trying not to show her tears.

Stan rubbed his hands across her back and looked down at her face. 'You alright?' he asked, sounding concerned.

'I, I need to...' Petra trailed off and began to sniff, as she wiped a lonely tear from her eye.

'What's the matter, darling?' Stan said, getting really worried now.

Petra composed herself and forced a smile. 'I need to go back to the ship now, darling, I don't want our last day or two ruined by this gloomy weather,' she said, uncoupling from him and sliding her hand into his.

Stan breathed a sigh of relief. 'Phew, for a minute there I thought someone had died.' He squeezed her hand.

Petra gave a nervous laugh and swung her handbag over her shoulder, and sidled in close to Stan as they made their way back to the ship. Her mind was awash with different scenarios that played out on how to tell Stan of Heparin's fate.

But the time to break the news clearly wasn't now.

8

RUSSIAN ROULETTE

The *AUGUR II*, sticking as close to the island as it could possibly get, cut great swathes through the tumultuous ocean.

The magnificent cruise ship shone bright in the fading darkness, as it made its way steadily onwards to its final destination. It tacked left and right to avoid the storm-driven sea that was silently building in momentum.

Stan stood at the window of his cabin, watching the island fade from view as the darkness took hold. He had just finished pulling his tie up tight against his collar when Petra exited the bathroom.

Petra approached him, looking radiant as her makeup and dress complemented her look.

'Pregnancy suits you. You look like you're blossoming,' Stan commented, pulling on his tuxedo jacket.

'Well I don't feel like it! I've got stretch marks all around my waist under this dress. No amount of cream or blemisher can hide them,' she said flatly.

'Well, you look lovely to me, however you feel,' Stan said, patting down his jacket to make sure his wallet was in his pocket.

'I'm not really feeling up to dining out tonight, Stan. Can't we just get room service and cuddle up and watch a movie on the TV?' Petra said, feeling the grooves of the marks around her waist.

'Seriously? It's our last night together on holiday. Tomorrow we will make land and it will be back to reality. I thought we could have one last memorable night to cherish,' Stan said, feeling deflated.

Petra looked at him with a saddened expression, crossing her arms above her swollen belly. 'I need to tell you something, Stan. I can't keep it to myself anymore!'

Stan looked puzzled. 'You're not carrying twins, are you?'

Petra sat down on the edge of the bed and beckoned Stan to join her.

'If it's about my little turn earlier today, darling, then I can assure you I'm fine. I will go for a check-up when—'

'It's Heparin!' Petra blurted out. She grabbed Stan's hand as he sat down and joined her.

'What about him?' Stan said, a lump appearing in his throat.

'There's no way to break it to you, Stan,' Petra said, fighting back the tears.

Stan looked at her warily.

'No! Not Hep! He was fine when we left a couple of weeks ago,' Stan said solemnly, reading Petra's body language.

Petra squeezed his hand tight and sobbed. 'I'm sorry Stan, but he's, he's... dead,' Petra trailed off.

Stan looked at her dumbfounded and in shock. 'Why? But... how?'

Petra looked at her husband and the tears rolled freely down her cheeks. 'He... was poisoned,' she said with her voice breaking off.

Stan gave a stony silence.

'I had missed calls from the girls whilst we were at port. They were in the vets when I got back to them,' Petra trailed off again.

'What? You mean he died whilst you were on the phone and you didn't think to tell me? Now I know why you seemed off, it all makes sense,' Stan said, the reality sinking in and anger surfacing in his tone.

'No, I had a choice to make. We could have tried keeping him alive until you and I got back. Or do the right thing to put him out of his suffering! ...I chose to put him under, Stan. I'm... so sorry!' Petra said, putting her arm around him.

Stan was speechless. He pulled away from his wife and went to the minibar. He opened the door but found it depleted of any stock. His mind raced as he tried to make sense of what she was saying.

Petra sat on the bed shaking and sniffing.

Stan slammed the fridge door and made Petra jump. 'Who the hell are you to make a decision like that?' Stan yelled with tears forming in the corner of his eyes.

'The girls rang me in a panic, Stan. I couldn't let them make the decision,' Petra said pleadingly.

'So you thought you were the one to do it?' Stan said, pacing up and down like a caged bear. 'Who poisoned him? Why would anyone do that?'

'I'm sorry, Stan. I'm so sorry,' Petra whimpered.

Stan looked at his wife with burning hatred. 'The choice should have been mine and mine alone!' Stan roared.

With that, he shot Petra a dark look and made for the door, yanking it open in a rage.

Petra cried out after him, but he had disappeared through and slammed it shut behind.

*

Stan staggered to the stairwell and began his descent down to deck 5. He was overcome with anger and emotion at only now realising his beloved cat was no more.

The numbers of each level passed in a blur as he slid along the stairwell wall further and further down. It was like his mood was sinking into despair with every step down that he took.

The sign for deck 5 honed into view as Stan navigated the last bend and traversed the steps. He pushed open the door from the foyer and found himself out on deck. He was greeted with a slight rocking motion from the steady increase of waves as they buffeted the ship.

With only one thing on his mind, he made his way to the bar where he ordered a double whiskey and sank it straight down with feeling of resentment and anger. A few more shots later and the waiter began to give him a funny look, or so it seemed. Stan decided he would make his way through to the adjoining casino.

Pulling out his wallet, Stan produced a twenty and exchanged it for an equivalent worth of chips.

He then made his way over to the roulette table. A svelte blonde woman was waiting there.

When the croupier saw Stan she smiled incredulously at him.

He looked at her name badge indiscreetly to get a reading on her name. He realised she was a buxom lady who was wearing a plunging neckline blouse with her breasts bursting from within, the badge almost bursting from her large bosom. He figured the better the looking croupier, the more money men would spend at the table. He wasn't going to be suckered in, not today.

'Hi. Serafima, is it? I'd like to place a wager please?' Stan said, feeling slightly abashed.

The croupier in her brazen Russian accent, directed him to the wheel and asked what he would like to wager.

Stan took in the roulette betting board and placed all his chips in one go. He had put a few on red 7, his lucky number. A stack on black 20 to give him luck for his twentieth anniversary, and the rest he randomly put on black 6 just for the hell of it.

Happy that all bets were placed, Serafina spun the wheel and flicked the yellow ball onto its track. Stan looked on, as the wheel span and a feeling of nausea washed over him. A sharp pain stabbed at the back of his eyes as the ball settled on black 6.

The croupier congratulated him and cleared the board.

Stan used his winning chips and placed them all on black 6. He felt unsteady on his feet and gripped hard on the table as the wheel was spun again and the ball was added.

Again, the ball nestled into black 6. Stan couldn't believe his fortune.

Petra must be wrong about Heparin, he thought.

Serafina looked on in amazement, she couldn't believe Stan's good luck either.

This American roulette wheel very rarely paid out, Serafina knew only too well. Especially for an amateur like the gentleman in front of her. If it was a European wheel then she could understand some degree of luck, as it was well known that you would fare better on them.

Stan felt the odd sensation of his tickly brain again. He tried to block it out as he squinted at the board. He placed all his chips on low black 6 again and waited.

The croupier went through the motions again, eyeing the black 6 nervously.

This time though, the ball went to settle on red 7. Serafina breathed a sigh of relief but suddenly a jolt from the ships aft pinged the ball from its resting place and it skipped over into black 6.

Serafina gasped.

Stan hadn't noticed though, as the jolt had sent him flying into a nearby stool where he knocked it over onto its side.

He didn't know what was going on. He picked himself up and staggered off away from the casino, leaving the croupier speechless, and back through to the bar, to make his way out to the open deck. He felt stifled and seriously needed air. Just then he thought he saw Heparin. The shadow of his cat ran past and it startled him, but at the same time Stan had an overwhelming urge to pursue it.

A feeling of calm and warmth washed over him, or it could be his relapse again. He wasn't sure. Fumbling for the hand rails, he gave chase, sliding himself along in the general direction the ghostly shadow had taken.

It appeared to his right and darted off into the foyer and off into the open lift.

Stan raced after it.

The doors slid shut behind him. A button had already been depressed for level 13 even though the lift was empty.

The elevator's overhead light, popped its bulb and bathed him in darkness.

Stan shot forward to feel the crack in the opposite doors, that would open on the other side when he reached his destination, knowing it would open onto the corridor for his cabin's level.

Finding it, he felt some small relief. His eyes started to adjust as he scanned for the cat.

Stan saw the shape of Heparin in the corner and immediately bent down to scoop up his beloved moggy but the overhead light fizzled back to life and then went out, plunging him into darkness again, making him disorientated, as the lift steadily ascended.

'Hep, Heparin!' he shouted after the silhouette that had blended into the darkness. Stan frantically fumbled around in the dark for the moggy for what seemed like an age.

Coming to rest on floor 13, the lift's doors opened and the moonlight came flooding in from a nearby window. The shape had gone and Stan couldn't believe that he had scrabbled around in the darkness in a frenzied state.

The corridor leading to his cabin ahead, too, was in darkness. Stan was afraid his mind was playing tricks on him as he caught sight of a large mass of darkness on the floor up ahead.

Then the ghost of the cat darted out in front of him and veered left, lit up by the pale moonlight. Stan was startled.

Again, he gave chase on an interconnecting corridor that bore left away from the dark mass. He had an overpowering urge to see Heparin one last time.

Further up ahead he saw the cat, his cat, he was sure, that looked at him with its bright green slitted eyes.

It made a dash for the heavy-set metal door that acted as a barrier to the outdoor deck. Stan thought he had it cornered but it passed through the door and out of sight. Stan lurched into action and burst through the door, bathed in the eerie glow that greeted him.

The door swung shut with a thud behind him.

Up ahead was Heparin sitting on a handrail licking his fur. Stan went to make a grab for him, just as another jolt from a large wave hitting the ship knocked him off his feet.

Stan went head first over the slippery railing and fell two floors.

A lifeboat that was swinging violently against the ship's rocking motions captured Stan as he smacked down onto its stretched orange tarp. The weight of Stan hitting the tarpaulin ripped it in two as he passed through and into its hold, smacking his head on the wooden seating.

Then he blacked out.

The spectre of Heparin plucked and pawed at the tarpaulin, then jumped down into the darkness of the hold to be reunited with his master.

9

HARD LABOUR

Petra had gone to look for her husband. She still wore her blue dress with the daisy patterns on it, but had concealed the dress with her blazer.

She had sat dazed and confused by what had happened earlier. Her blood pressure was rising and it made her feel giddy.

She wiped away her tears and snatched up her cigarettes from under the pillow. She was made of sterner stuff than this and she vowed to get a grip on herself.

Petra was determined to make things right between her and Stan. She knew he could be a stubborn son of a bitch, but she also knew that he would come round soon enough.

As Petra made her way down the corridor to the elevator, she passed by some concerned-looking passengers who were deep in conversation about the worrying turn of events of the storm that was now upon them. Petra had been so wrapped up in her own thoughts earlier, that she barely registered the announcement from the captain that the *Augur II* was sailing into troubled waters. She was more concerned with her own troubles with Stan, than the ship's dangerous predicament.

There were some bulletin messages about staying, or returning to your cabin for safety reasons and a meeting taking place in the muster stations located around many hotspots of the vessel, but she hadn't paid them much notice.

She mildly heard a faint bulletin "that in the event of a whiteout by the spray from the sea and a gale force storm, evacuation could be on the cards as they were too far out at sea!"

But she was still too distraught to pay it any heed. The only thing she made sense of was that the captain was over-apologetic that he had gone into the heart of the storm that raged suddenly from out of nowhere.

Petra knew what she was doing was against all hers and Stan's beliefs. She could hear Stan now in his accusing tone. 'Don't put yourself, or our son's safety in any danger to come looking for me.' But she was worried sick. Never before had Stan worked himself up into quite the state as he had this evening. It was much worse than what had happened down by the river a couple of years ago.

Petra had barely made it to the lift, when an onset of nausea overcame her. She wasn't sure if it was the motion of the sea or something worse. She steadied her hand against the wall and put her other hand over her mouth for fear of actually being sick.

As if out of nowhere a large wave crashed into the ship and the jolt sent her flying sideways along the wall, knocking the wind out of her as she fell hard to the floor.

Screaming out in agony, she reeled in pain and

clutched at her stomach, unaware of the hidden damage that had now surfaced, brought on by her high blood pressure.

Still clutching her stomach, Petra struggled to her feet and dragged herself to the lift doors. She reached out and pressed the call button.

It was then she realised there was a wet sensation trickling down her thigh. 'Oh God, something's wrong,' Petra muttered under her breath.

She reached into her blazer pocket to pull out her phone but only found her packet of cigarettes. She crumpled them in her fist, as a stabbing sensation crippled her abdomen.

Turning from the still-closed lift doors and the slow climbing elevator, Petra hobbled back towards her cabin in a panic. In her haste to find Stan she had forgotten to retrieve her phone from the side cabinet.

Discarding the crumpled packet, she fell to the floor again in agony and grabbed her crotch.

Pulling her sodden hand away in horror, she realised it was stained in her blood.

Then the lights went out, surrounding her in darkness. She heard the elevator door swish open and someone exit it, but she was too afraid to cry out.

When the emergency lighting finally kicked in she found herself face to face with a young woman who had left her cabin with a sense of curiosity on hearing the commotion from the hall way.

The young woman knelt down beside Petra with concern on her face and realised quite quickly that the middle aged, but very beautiful pregnant lady before her, seriously needed medical aid.

*

The first responder, Tanya, was called along with Doctor Erikson and Petra found herself loaded onto a stretcher, being hastily carted off to the infirmary.

'You've lost a lot of blood, Mrs Palmer,' Doctor Erikson said gravely. 'I'm afraid I don't have the resources on board to deal effectively with your condition. I have made arrangements with the captain in the bridge to have you flown to land by the ship's helicopter from the landing pad, just as soon as the storm has passed,' he said as they hurried along.

Holding onto both handles at the foot end of the stretcher, doctor Erikson shot Tanya, who was carrying Petra's head end, a grave look.

They had recently exited the elevator and were working their way through the corridors, but the motion of the rocking ship had thrown them off balance and on numerous occasions they were buffeted off the high-sheen glossed walls.

Petra, becoming delirious, called out for Stan but was shushed by the nurse Tanya.

'You need bed rest, but first we need to know where your husband is, Mrs Palmer?' Doctor Erikson said in a grunt, as he wrestled to keep a firm grip on the handles.

'I don't know, we had a fight... he stormed off,' Petra said, through laboured breathing.

'Did HE do this to you?' Tanya asked, concerned.

'NO... God, no, the storm threw me into the wall... Please find him? I need him now... I need...' Petra trailed off.

'We will, I promise,' Tanya said, steering the stretcher around a bend.

'I will send word once we stabilise you, but I'm

afraid my first concern is you, Mrs Palmer,' Doctor Erikson interjected. 'My diagnosis is that you have pre-eclampsia, Mrs Palmer, and I'm really worried for you, but we need to test your urine first and get a blood test. We don't have the facilities here to deal with this. We must get you stable and ready to fly as soon as this damn weather has cleared.'

Petra's head rolled to the side as she doubled up in pain. 'My baby! Will my baby be okay?' Petra pleaded as she pulled her arms in tight around her stomach.

Both doctor and nurse exchanged troubled looks. With all that was happening right now, neither one of them could possibly give a comforting answer. At best Petra Palmer would pull through this. At worst her baby's life might be in serious jeopardy. One thing was certain, though. There was going to be serious overtime invested by both doctor and nurse; their laborious work was going to be stretched.

For them it would be a serious graft to stabilise Petra with little resources and they knew they would experience hard labour in doing so.

10

THE INTRAVENOUS INTERVENTION

As Petra lay in one of the six beds in the infirmary, hooked up to an intravenous drip, Tanya checked her temperature and put the palm of her hand to Petra's forehead.

'She is feverish and clammy to the touch! What course of action should we take, Doctor Erikson, sir?' Tanya said concerned, as she also noticed how swollen their patient was around the face and hands.

Doctor Erikson, who was in talks with two male nurses discussing Petra's options, turned to Tanya and hesitated.

'We are beyond giving her aspirin, I'm afraid. All we can do is make Mrs Palmer comfortable as we can't interfere further. Because we don't have the facilities, I don't want to try anything too risky anyway. So the only option now we have established it is pre-eclampsia, is to monitor her closely until this storm passes. I pray Mrs Palmer's condition does not worsen. The captain is doing his best to get us out of the storm. He said he will notify me of any developments.'

'Yes of course, I understand,' Tanya said.

'Jorge here has taken a blood sample from Mrs Palmer but it's not good. She has a rare blood type, AB negative. We will have to find a matching donor, but the chances are slim. Until then, there is not much else we can do,' Doctor Erikson said coolly.

Tanya noted that the doctor had sweat collecting in the folds of his wrinkled forehead and that his demeanour did not match his character. They were going to be in for a rough ride.

'Okay, I agree. We do what we can, without complicating matters. Let's hope we can keep her stabilised without any further complications arising then,' Tanya said doubtfully.

*

Before Petra succumbed to the blurring darkness that came to her in bouts, a spectrum of twinkly lit stars sparkled across her vision. She blinked against them as they bore deep within her brain. She likened them to a firework sparkler that had been thrust into her face, the sparkling and crackling of each star burning her retina, fizzing on contact with each strike.

Then a feeling of serenity washed over her as the darkness smothered her whole. She became unconscious.

When she blinked her eyes again, a pale blue light came into focus and she found herself staring through a film of gellified water.

She brought her hands up in front of her face and realised she was cocooned in the stuff.

In a blind panic she tried to swipe it away but found it sticky and clotted to the touch.

Petra then became aware that she was moving at a

fast pace and that in actual fact she was on her back sliding downwards at a rate of knots.

Thrusting her arms wide, she tried to slow down and halt her descent but the gelatinous substance held her fast. It was like she had awoken in suspended animation.

Squirming against her oppressive state, she tried to call out but to her horror, felt that her throat was lined with the gunk. It made her gag at the thought of not getting air.

Suddenly and without warning, she felt herself free like she was flying, briefly followed by a large splash that hit her with full force.

Again, she twisted and convulsed to rid herself of her oppressive shackles, as a sinking feeling took hold.

Eventually the gel-like substance began to disperse all around her, slowly being replaced by a lukewarm sensation of water that rushed into her lungs, giving her a brief feeling of euphoria before realisation overwhelmed her.

Petra's screams were replaced by gargles as the water cleared the gunk from her mouth that had slowly begun to drown her.

With a defiant rage, she kicked and lashed out, finding herself free and floating in a large body of water.

She looked around in fright, spotting light radiating overhead.

With a sense of urgency and bewilderment she found the use of her limbs and swam upwards to what she hoped was the surface, air and freedom.

Petra emerged into a breathtaking vista.

She found that she was in the centre of a large pool. Behind her rose a sheer cliff face that climbed upwards. It housed a cavernous hole a third of the way up, that seemed to be the exit she had ejected from. Oozing from the hole, was the pale blue gel that had formed into stalactites clinging onto the rocky surface around the rim.

She looked back round, astonished at what had happened. Before her was a lush green embankment, peppered with wild daisies. Beyond that lay a pebbled path stretching off through a thicket of trees, with a further path veering off and snaking away through a narrow gorge.

Petra made for the bank and pulled herself up and out, still coughing from the rush of air she had exhaled on surfacing the pool. She pulled herself unsteadily to her feet and saw she was still in her daisy-patterned dress and royal blue blazer.

The clothing, wet from the pool, clung to her body and made her shiver, sending goosebumps along her pale arms and legs.

A harsh cold wind swept across her and whistled through the trees up ahead.

Petra thought that she was in a dream, as it was the only sensible thought that had occurred to her. Being a neurologist made her always rationalise the brain's ever-complex reasoning.

She made for the pebbled path and looked down to her bare feet. Something didn't seem right to her. Then it came to her in a flash; she could see her feet. *I must be dreaming as I'm not pregnant anymore,* she thought.

It made her feel a little better about herself as it had to be a dream after all, but she still couldn't fathom why a dream would make you think about reality like that.

Petra shrugged off the feeling and made her way across the path.

The small pebbles scrunched and squeaked as her feet dispersed them underfoot and she made her way on, telling herself over and over that she would wake any minute, to find that all was okay with her and her baby.

The path wound on throughout the dense population of trees, until Petra found herself at the crest of a wooden suspension bridge which crossed a large gully of sea below. The gully was a narrow channel that cut through both rock faces and in the near distance she could make out a sand bank-like path from somewhere off to the bridge's side exit below. It met a small barren island of sand nestling in the sea.

The bridge's span was at least a hundred feet long and swayed side to side, creaking as the wind whistled through its planks and rope railings.

Petra was about to give up and turn around to head back the way she had come, when a baby's cry wailed off in the distance from below the bridge.

The wind contorted the baby's cry and it sent a shiver down Petra's spine.

A longing for motherhood again or the sense of being alone gave Petra a new steely determination and she turned back to the rickety bridge. She didn't know if it was curiosity or something else, but she knew she had to find out where the sound was coming from.

She took tentative steps and crossed out onto the threshold.

The wind whipped her dark brown hair across her face and blew icy cold through her very soul, as she delicately pulled her way across. Part of her realised that she shouldn't be experiencing these sensations in a dream, but still she pressed on.

Her teeth chattered and she shivered against the cold. Again, this experience in a dream shouldn't be had, she told herself over and over.

Finally she found herself more than halfway across.

Craning her neck, she strained to hear the crying that had been silenced by the gale-force wind which superseded it since she had stepped foot on the bridge.

Nothing.

A rotten plank creaked underneath her and her heart quickened.

She became afraid that it might give way any time soon, so she started off again with more urgency.

Petra didn't notice the approaching figure at the bridge exit as she was too busy staring down at her footing on each plank to focus on anything else.

'Well, aren't you a sight for sore eyes, my little daisy?' the ominous figure bellowed across the buffeting wind.

Petra looked up, startled and frightened, almost losing her footing through a gap between two planks. Nathaniel honed into view, his half-regenerated wings dragging behind him. He beckoned Petra into his waiting arms.

Once Petra realised who it was she didn't feel quite so scared anymore. 'Now I know I'm dreaming,' she said, exasperated.

'Is that any way to go about greeting me?' Nathaniel

boomed.

Petra looked on, astonished. 'I'm sorry, but you're dead. You died long ago, Dad, what are you doing here?' she replied, shouting into the wind in disbelief.

Nathaniel reached out to his daughter and again beckoned her in close for a big bear hug.

'Come to me, my little daisy. I've missed you so much, my fragile little flower.'

Petra approached him warily, the warning message from an unconscious Stan earlier now buzzing in her head.

This was a manifestation, for that she was sure.

No harm would come to her. This was only a dream, she reminded herself.

'I've missed you too, Dad,' she said, welling up, throwing her arms around his waist.

Father and daughter were reunited once more as Nathaniel reciprocated, bringing his mangled wings round to shelter his daughter from the harsh winds.

Petra paid little notice to his wings, as she was swept up in past longing to see her dad once more.

Her heavenly angel of a father that she must have dreamed up for comfort, in her most harrowing of circumstances, was obviously her brain's coping mechanism to deal with the stress that her body was going through.

11

GRAVE DANGER

Stan awoke with a start and found himself on his back, still dressed in his tuxedo, rocking gently in a row boat. The boat's tarpaulin was smothering him and he wrestled to remove it from his obscured vision.

Flipping onto his front, he pulled his legs in underneath him and forced himself up.

He removed the stretched tarp that had collapsed in on him. Fighting with it, he cast it aside. It flapped against a strong wind and was whipped away before splashing down into the flowing river, the gaping rip swallowing up the water as it sunk from view.

Stan became unsteady on his feet, as he struggled to maintain his balance against the choppy water that battered the boat.

It was then that it hit him. The boat was adrift on a river in a long, high, cavernous tunnel with its only source of light off in the distance accompanied by a roaring sound.

He wasn't on board the *Augur II* anymore.

Stan fell to his knees in shock as he adjusted to his surroundings. Panic and fear rushed in.

He looked behind him into the blanket of darkness and realised where he now was.

Somehow he had ended up back within his mind, but not how he had encountered this place before. He didn't know how he knew, but somehow he just did.

All thoughts of his past encounters in the oasis of his mind's unconscious state back when he was in his coma, came back to him in a haze.

Sitting himself down upon the wooden seat, Stan gripped both sides of the gunwale as the fear of why he was back came flooding over him. Was he dead this time? Or was he in yet another coma? Then it dawned on him. Lysis' warning earlier on board the *Augur II*! That was why he was back. Lysis had sent for him somehow, sending him a message from this world of his imagination to the one of his reality.

Stan cradled his head in his hands. If Lysis had sent for him, how come his reality and his unconsciousness had melded into one another? He knew he had to find Lysis for answers.

What was Lysis' warning? Something about being aware of Nathaniel and how he will take what Stan holds dear.

Stan found himself now gripping at his tie with shallow breaths.

What if he couldn't go back this time? What if this nightmare followed him back if he did return?

'Lysis? Lysis, it's me, Stan, where are you?' he shouted through the gloom.

All that greeted him was his empty-sounding echoes that resounded off the glistening, wet cave structure.

Stan kicked out in frustration and knocked against something with his foot. Whatever it was thudded against the wooden hull.

Stan reached over and seized the object, pulling it up close for inspection. It was a wooden oar, albeit one that had seen better days. Now it was weather-beaten and the paddle was gorged in places.

Stan laid it back down and searched around for a second one, but he came back empty handed.

Figuring one oar was enough, Stan held it aloft again and began to row towards the light, changing sides to keep the boat on an even keel.

As he neared the tunnel's opening, the light became clearer, illuminating the floor of the boat.

Gasping in astonishment, Stan made out that he was not alone in the boat. There at the stern was the adult form of Heparin, who once realising Stan had spotted him, gave a pitiful meow and decided to venture over. Stan wept with joy as he dropped the oar to the deck and picked up his loud purring companion and hugged him tight.

All time seemed to stand still as Stan nuzzled in to Heparin's fur, elating him in joy and sadness that they should be reunited under these circumstances. Stan then knew it to be true, Heparin had indeed passed from life.

The elated moment was short-lived, however, as the boat sailed out through the mouth of the tunnel and the cascading, freezing cold waterfall curtain from above showered them both.

Heparin shrieked in terror, scratched at Stan's face and turned tail, leaping through the curtain and out onto an adjacent bank through the other side, as Stan failed to keep a hold of him.

The boat quickly filled up with water and Stan, wet

and miserable, found himself waist high in a sinking boat that then capsized as he struggled to exit, the one remaining oar floating off down river into the distance.

Stan pulled himself out of the drink and crawled over to the cat who was licking himself with one leg in the air on the grassy bank.

Smiling at Heparin, Stan pulled up and stroked him, looking around as he wrung the water from his tie.

He and Heparin were back in the oasis of hope once more. In the sinkhole that had blossomed over time to reflect Stan's mind. The place Lysis resided over.

*

Heparin kept looking back at Stan as he slinked through the long grass, occasionally leaping out at unsuspecting butterflies to swat and play with. He had fully matured now, but old age would not befall him as he sensed that this was to be his only sanctuary from now on. But Heparin didn't mind. Here he could do much more than was possible with the short life he had experienced back there in physical existence.

Heparin soon lost interest with his playthings though, and stalked off over to a place between two boulders, that were half submerged in the river bed. He spotted Lysis pinned there, but gave no notice as a large koi swam into view, distracting him.

The cat leaned over the river bank's edge and pawed at the surface, taunted by the silver and yellow ghost koi, swimming in an arc below.

Stan looked upwards to the heavens and saw what he could only describe as an eclipse, half hidden by the ridge. There in the night sky it hovered, a full blood-red moon with a halo of light around its circumference. Turning his attention from its magnificence for not knowing what it could mean, Stan made his way over to Heparin and caught sight of Lysis pinned to the river bed.

Stan, mortified and in sheer terror, jumped into the river in haste and went blindly splashing over to Lysis' aid.

He squatted down at the head of Lysis and brought the coffin fly's head up to the surface in his cradling arms.

'Lysis! My god. What's happened to you? Who did this to you?' he screamed.

Lysis, as if jolted from a nightmare, spat out a stream of water and retched for air. 'Stan, I had hoped you'd come,' he said through a hoarse voice.

'We need to get you out of here, what should I do?' Stan asked pleadingly.

'Tap... into your potential, Stan, harness... your power and set me... free,' Lysis said, battling for breath.

Stan didn't know what Lysis was referring to so he began to scour his surroundings. He spotted the floating oar that had done a full lap of the circular river and then to the upturned boat nearby.

'That's it, I can use the oar. Look I'm going to prop your head up with the boat and use the oar to pry the boulders off your wings. Just give me a minute okay?' Stan said, eager that he had found a simple solution.

He dropped Lysis' head and went floundering off.

'Stan. Use your inner power!' Lysis shouted, straining to keep his head above water, now that Stan had wandered off. 'You have gotten stronger since returning here, you just don't know it yet,' he added, using his one good eye to keep a track on Stan. 'It's because your life in reality is failing, that you are increasing in strength here. You just don't know it yet,' Lysis croaked, just before his head fell below the surface again.

Stan, who had his back to Lysis, was too busy trying to manoeuvre the capsized boat into position, to listen fully to what he was saying.

'Yeah, that's fine. Understood. Now hold on a minute while I just drag this here,' Stan said, grunting and groaning, bringing the boat to Lysis' head.

Stan kneed the boat in and pulled Lysis' head to the surface and placed it on the curvature of the boat's hull.

'Stan, listen to me,' Lysis said weakly.

'Hold that thought, dear friend,' Stan said, as he splashed off noisily to retrieve the oar, dispersing the nearby fish.

Lysis' protests went unheard, as Stan came back with the oar and proceeded to use it to jimmy off one of the boulders.

He wedged the paddle as close to the underside of the boulder as he could and used all his force and might to push the handle down.

But with a deafening crack, the oar snapped in two, sending Stan face-down into the watery depths.

Stan came back up for air cursing and swearing. 'I'm sorry Lysis, I will try something else. I promise.'

'No time, Stan. Listen to me... please,' Lysis said with a saddened tone.

Stan splashed the water in frustration and approached his friend in distress.

'Okay. I'm listening,' Stan said defeatedly.

'Death will come for you, Stan. It has always been the will of the ones that oversee all we do. I was entrusted by them to bring you here the first time as I have done now. Through deception and will, it has always been my doing and for that I am truly sorry. This place will soon fade from existence and you will be all that remains of it. This is all in your mind. When you pass over here permanently this place will be no more. They have greater plans for you, but this part of your journey is necessary for you to accept your true calling, do you understand?'

Stan looked at Lysis with dismay. 'So I'm going to die?' he said flatly.

'Everyone dies, Stan, and most don't get a warning, but you can make a difference before that happens, which is why I brought you here. They may not like my defiance but I am willing to sacrifice myself for the cause in order for you to become the man I hope you would be,' Lysis said, fixing his bad eye on Stan.

'But I'm going to die... I can't! not yet! I'm not ready! You say I have a power, what is it? Is it power to live?' Stan said, putting his hands in his pockets.

'You imagine this place in your mind. There are countless places like this that belong to other people, but this is yours. You can manipulate this landscape just by willing it to change. Sure, there is an evil that doesn't obey the rules that you cannot influence, but this space around you is your weapon to help vanquish them. You just need to believe in yourself, but I am afraid it will not stop your destiny.'

'And what evil do I face this time that bears any resemblance to preventing my fate from happening or slowing it down?' Stan said defiantly.

'Nothing that will aid you, I'm afraid, Stan. Your destiny is already set in stone.'

'So what's the point then? Why should I bother?' Stan said, watching Heparin pouncing on a large koi that was flapping about on dry land.

'Because it involves your unborn son and that of your wife, Petra!' Lysis said with dismay.

This seemed to change Stan's gloomy mood. 'What of them, Lysis? WHAT OF THEM?' Stan demanded.

'Nathaniel, your deceased father-in-law. He has been exiled from beyond the veil. He wishes to be born again and start anew. He is seeking reincarnation,' Lysis said, allowing Stan to take the statement in.

'You don't mean...'

'Yes, Stan. He wishes to possess your unborn son here, to have the chance of a second life there, of materiality. Without Petra remembering what has happened here when she finally gets back home, no one can stop him.'

Stan stroked his chin, deep in thought. 'So if I can defeat him here then he won't be a concern to my family. Seeing how he died years ago, I think I can deal with that,' Stan said, weighing in.

'But there is a larger and more real concern, Stan!' Lyis said.

'That is?'

'Your wife has already crossed over here with your

son and Nathaniel has already plotted to make his move.'

Stan swivelled round to face Lysis and stared at him in disbelief. 'How? She was fine when I left her on board. Well, maybe not fine, as we had an argument, but her wellbeing was fine anyway. I can't see how that is even possible!'

'Shortly after you stormed out, Stan, she suffered pre-eclampsia. Right now, she is fighting for her life and your son's, back on board the ship in freak weather, whilst you are unconscious in a lifeboat dangling precariously over the side of it.'

'Great, so here we go again then. Up the ante and let Stan deal with it. So where are they around here then?' Stan said, throwing his hands to the sky.

'Across the ocean at Petra's own oasis.'

'So how do we get there?' Stan said, wading in circles.

'Well it's clear that you cannot harness your power yet, so either you find it quick and release me, or you resort to ripping off my wings so I can be free of this temporary prison. Unless of course you detest me that much that you choose to go it alone.'

'I may not understand you wholly, Lysis, but I do need your help. It's clear that my wife and child are in grave danger, so how do I free you with this untapped power?' Stan said, feeling anxious.

'You can't right away, but with my tuition, then you can soon. Just not yet. I suggest we do that when we are well on our way. I need you to grab that split oar and smash off my wings.'

'You what! I don't know if I can do that,' Stan said, looking concerned.

'You have to, it just means I will never fly again.'

'But if I get better then you will regenerate. Like we did before,' Stan said, looking hopeful.

'There's no coming back from this, Stan. This will be a one-way trip for the both of us. We are both on borrowed time. For you, you will be on a half life,' Lysis said solemnly.

'A half life?'

'A last chance to put your affairs in order. Because if anything happens to you in your world from now on, there will be no going back to it once you end up here again. Here you will stay for eternity, unless you earn your wings,' Lysis said, then added, 'now remove my wings so we can be on our way, dear friend.'

Stan looked at his reflection in the muddy water, lost in thought.

'Wait a second. So how much danger is Petra in? On board the ship, I mean... Lysis?' Stan enquired, changing the subject.

'If we can intercept the reincarnation and get you all home safely, then all that will remain is for you to give her some of your blood, for that is what she will need in your world to survive this ordeal.'

'You mean she needs a transfusion?' Stan said with realisation dawning on him.

'Yes, your blood. You both have the same blood type if I am not mistaken. The very rare AB negative! If you fail to reach her in time then I don't need to tell you what will become of her too,' Lysis said, straining to look into Stan's eyes.

'So I need to stop an evil possession and get back to my wife to save her life!' Stan said, eyeing Heparin, who had set about devouring the koi.

'Yes, I am afraid so, but there is more at play here than just that. I need to be freed first, so we can plan accordingly.'

'Okay, I just need a minute to focus before we do this,' Stan said urgently, grief-stricken at the thought of the mighty task ahead.

Stan approached the wings shimmering beneath the surface and each of the boulders they were pinned to.

He retrieved the oar and picked up the paddle end, turning it over in his hands, and raised it above his head.

He felt sick at the very thought of harming his friend, but he realised that he had no other options open to him.

He bit down on his bottom lip and brought the oar down with a squint in his eyes at what he was about to do.

The deafening screams of Lysis echoed around the oasis, sending animals and birds scattering far and wide as the splintered oar tore through the wing's membrane.

Heparin's ears pricked up and looked on, startled.

He didn't know what all the fuss was about, so turned his attention back to his half-eaten fish.

12

THE DAISY CHAIN

Petra, having been led by her dad to the secret meadow sanctuary of her mind, gazed around in awe.

The large mesh of conifers sheltered the pair from the prevailing winds that, with force, bent the tips of the conifers over. The wind whistled overhead, forcing Petra to speak louder than usual. 'So you're telling me this is my safe place and that it's all in my mind, but not like a dream. More of a coping mechanism that I have imagined to shelter me from the harsh realities of life, which is just as I thought. An unconscious state that once I have woken up from, will soon be forgotten about, right?'

Nathaniel was sitting within the ring of daisies on the earthly mound, feeding the discarded daisy chain through his fingers.

He smiled briefly, it was just like his daughter to over-rationalise and bombard him with the facts. His smile waned and he was momentarily lost in thought, as if something was missing, but he couldn't put his finger on it.

'I know it's hard to believe. Trust me! But it's all true. When you die, you eventually end up in a place like this. Here to serve as a guardian to another soul on Earth, until you have earned the right to own your wings and then you will move on. This astral plane is like a stepping stone to something greater. It took me a long time to adjust, but for you now, this is just a glimpse at what will come.'

Petra looked on disbelievingly. 'It's a very colourful notion for sure, but come on, as if?' she said, placing her hands upon her waist.

'Okay, fine. I see you need more proof. The bridge you crossed earlier, did you notice the path below made of sand that cut through the ocean to a small outcrop of a small isle?'

Petra nodded. 'It's where I heard a baby's cry come from.'

'Yes, it belongs to your unborn baby, whose island is now forming and linked to yours. His oasis to be. When he comes of birth age the sand bank that connects the two of you will be covered by the sea. On his birth, his mind will develop along with the island and it will take on his persona, if you will.'

Petra by now had sunk to her knees and was plucking at a daisy. Still she wasn't convinced.

She twirled the daisy in her fingers. 'It all sounds so incredible that I just can't believe what I'm hearing, Dad.'

Nathaniel placed the daisy garland over his neck and rose to his feet. 'Okay darling, then let me try to persuade you further,' he said.

Nathaniel stuck two fingers into his mouth and whistled. Within seconds Goliath came bounding over the gate and padded over to him, sitting down at his feet.

'Do you remember this lumbering brute by any chance?' Nathaniel said, running a hand through Goliath's fur.

In an instant Petra was beaming and all doubt had dissolved. 'Oh my god, Goliath,' she said, patting her knees.

Goliath looked from his master to Petra and he twitched his ears, then he sprang up and dashed over to Petra, plonking his heavy weight onto her.

They tussled playfully for a while before Goliath slouched down, enjoying having his belly rubbed.

Petra wiped her tears of joy away and picked up a nearby branch from a conifer, that had been wrenched free from the storm.

She stood up and looked to her dad, 'Will he still do the trick I taught him with the stick, Dad, I wonder?'

'I see no reason why not, love, go on and try it,' Nathaniel gestured as he spun the garland around his thick neck.

Petra bent the branch over her knee and forced it to snap, leaving it bent at a 45-degree angle. Then she jabbed one end of it into the earth.

'Come on then, boy, show me what you got,' she squealed, pointing to the 'R'-like shape of the stick in the ground.

Goliath paced around the stick and his ears went forward, then he bared his teeth at the branch and turned to Petra, growling, foam salivating at the corner of his jowls.

Petra, taken aback, started to back away, warding him off. 'What's going on Dad? What's the matter with him?' she said, sounding scared.

Nathaniel shot over to his daughter and stepped in front of her, acting as protection. 'I don't know, Petra, this isn't like him,' he said, stretching out his hands to the dog.

Goliath bared his teeth wider and thrashed his tail wildly, raising his rear up. He began to bark a deep guttural roar.

'Goliath, STOP NOW! That's enough!' Nathaniel roared.

The dog's eyes glazed over as it shimmered its fur.

Then it sprang at Nathaniel with its mouth open, trying to strike at his throat.

Nathaniel caught the dog mid-air, with his hands clamping around the vicious dog's neck.

Goliath sent Nathaniel onto his back and the towering beast snapped violently at his face.

Petra in alarm seized up the impaled branch and raced over to her father's aid, swinging the thick branch at the dog's hide.

But it was too late. The dog overpowered Nathaniel and bit down into his Adam's apple, crunching through the windpipe.

Arterial blood sprayed the mutt as it released its vice-like grip and turned, frothing at the mouth at Petra.

Nathaniel gripped his gashed throat, trying to stem the bleeding as he pulled himself over into the daisy circle, the whites of his eyes wide with terror.

He started scrabbling with his free hand at the dirt, trying to clear it away. Dreading the worst at what he would unearth, now realisation had crept in.

Blood gushed from him, staining the dirt mound

copper red, around him.

He tried to scream for Petra to run but the sweet taste of blood gurgled in his mouth, preventing him from doing so.

*

Hidden in a shallow grave, buried under a mound of earth in the centre of a ring of daisies, lay the mangled remains of Alcina, in the resting place she once called home at Petra's oasis.

The Tibetan mastiff, Goliath, had razored its way through Alcina's tender flesh like a rag doll being stripped of stuffing and buried her like a prized bone.

Dripping through the soil to Alcina's empty vessel trickled the blood of Nathaniel that began to seep new life into her hollow carcass.

Back in Petra's earthbound world, her postpartum haemorrhage began to take hold, as it reflected here and now in the secret meadow of her mind as a clot forming Thrombus.

*

Petra tried to get to her father as he lay bleeding out in the circle of daisies, but the mastiff Goliath, had cut off her entry and stood as a sentry growling at her.

Clamping a hand over her mouth, Petra sobbed.

Goliath then began to change before her very eyes, taking on a skeletal, winged, ghostly form. When the transition was complete the apparition turned to Petra and glared at her through a deathly stare.

'Who, who are you?' Petra gasped through hushed tones.

The spectral being knelt down at her father's side

and prodded him with a bony finger.

Nathaniel groaned and the abnormal form turned its head to face her. 'That doesn't matter, who I am. What does matter is that you do what I tell you to do, or you will suffer the same fate at as your father... little daisy,' it said with malice.

Petra gasped in horror.

The figure spoke again, but this time it sounded calculated and menacing. 'This ring of daisies is a border of a portal, or gateway if you prefer, that will return you back to your world. It would normally have a gatekeeper here to prevent guardians crossing over into your world whenever they seem fit, but as you can see, you do not have one, as I claimed her soul a while back. She is now buried under the mound that your father is bleeding all over,' it said, as it removed the blood-soaked garland of daisies from around Nathaniel's neck.

Petra stood motionless and glanced over her shoulder to the wooden gate.

The ghostly being stood up and from its back its wings spread out, casting a dark shadow across Petra. 'This garland I have in my possession is a crafted tether from this world to yours. When it is placed around my neck and yours, it will splice us together and all we have to do is step into the gateway so we can both return to your world, where you will have your life back and I can have life again, but in a new womb... your womb, to be precise.'

Petra began to back away as she tried to process what she was seeing and hearing.

The figure, sensing her motives, swooped across to the gate and barred her way.

'Not so fast, are we? What Nathaniel said is true for the best part of it, but he left out some damning details. You should not feel sorry for him as it was his intention to do just what I have discussed. Can you imagine raising your father as your son? No! That will not do at all... Instead you will raise me! I will meld with your unborn son's soul and we will share a life together raised by you, a wonderful mother that will have no knowledge of any of this lead-up of events ever taking place.'

Petra turned and ran to her father, pleading for him to help her out of this nightmare, not believing a word the winged creature was saying.

Nathaniel looked up to his daughter and grabbed her arm. 'I, I'm so sorry, my darling daughter, please forgive me,' he choked through the blood oozing from his lips.

Petra knelt over him and sobbed. 'Why, Daddy? Why did you want this to happen?' she wailed.

Nathaniel pulled her in close and whispered in her ear, 'You must help me, grab my sack of seagulls. They will rejuvenate me. I left them down by the bridge. I can stop this. I can make things...'

Petra was hauled off her dad and cast aside and Nathaniel was dragged out of the circle.

'Enough of this,' the entity said. 'You will join me under this garland now, as we must be on our way,' the creature said, offering Petra the garland of daisies. 'You will be reunited with your son, i.e. me, soon, when I am born. Also left here in your mind will be something that too will start to grow, something that will keep your husband occupied for a long time. My parting gift to him for allowing me a second chance...

Thrombus will be reborn!'

Nathaniel reeled in horror; he knew now what was going on under the soil he lay upon and that he had been a sacrificial pawn to make it happen. 'Why? Who are you?' he said through a bloody rasp.

But he already knew what the answer would be.

'But it's me, Nathaniel, your old apprentice. Your charge. You knew me as William Last, but I'm sure I will have a new name, soon,' it said, laughing hysterically.

'No, it can't be! Lysis said you were gone. How is this possible?' Nathaniel wailed as the blood congealed at his throat and his essence began to melt away.

13

UP THE CREEK WITHOUT A PADDLE

Lysis, having recovered from his ordeal, tried to block out the pain as he scaled the cliff face out from the oasis with his sticky feet in an erratic movement.

Stan watched him in amazement as he followed close behind, grief-stricken and remorse surging through him, as he gripped onto ledges with his fingers and placed his feet into nooks and crevices to boost himself higher.

Sitting at the peak in the tall grass, was Heparin, who had nimbly sprung from ledge to ledge and had made the summit in a short amount of time. He craned his neck and licked between his paw, whilst he waited.

'So we established how Goliath came to be guardian of my wife's oasis. But what of this Alcina? How did she become gatekeeper then, Lysis?' Stan said, jimmying along a narrow fissure.

Lysis looked down to Stan. 'Surely you are aware of Petra's fondness for Greek mythology, Stan?'

'Well, yes I suppose,' Stan said, as he found another

foothold. 'She always had her head in one book or another on those subjects, but I guess I've never given it much thought. Why?' Stan asked, stopping for breath.

'Well, Alcina was a sorceress that ruled over magical islands, who seduced passing sailors. But once she had grown bored of their company, she would turn them into animals,' Lysis said, swivelling his good eye back to look up.

'Okay, so Alcina is Petra's interpretation of a gatekeeper like you are mine then?'

'In a roundabout way, yes,' Lysis said as he reached the top to join Heparin.

Stan, who was only halfway up, stopped again. 'Okay, makes sense I guess,' he shouted up.

'I fear she isn't protecting your wife's oasis now and that troubles me dearly,' Lysis said matter-of-factly.

Stan wet his lips and was about to challenge Lysis, but decided against it.

'So anyway, how are you feeling now Lysis?' he shouted through shallow breaths, watching Lysis' tail slink over the lip.

'I'm not too bad' Stan. Luckily the pureness of the river has eased my severed stumps somewhat,' Lysis said, shouting down, whilst checking the remaining nubs at his back. 'If I get a phantom itch then I'm going to need you to help me scratch them,' he said jokingly.

Stan continued his ascent and finally made it up to the peak to join his companions.

After all Lysis had endured, he still had his humour. Stan was just glad that the healing properties of the oasis river had acted as analgesic to ease the shocking pain.

He flung his legs over the lip and looked down upon the oasis with sadness. 'Are you going to miss this place, old friend?' he said, getting his breath back.

'It has been my home for only a short time, Stan. I'm sure this feeling of anguish will pass,' Lysis said, turning away.

Stan got back to his feet and stroked Heparin behind the ears. 'You're getting bigger, I swear, Hep!' he said.

The cat regarded him for a minute, twitched his nose then padded off to join Lysis, leaving Stan to cast one last look.

The trio approached the row boat that was upright nestling on a flattened bush.

Heparin jumped in and Lysis looked to Stan. 'Ready?'

'As I'll ever be,' Stan said.

Lysis arched his back and pushed the flat aft of the boat with his head, as Stan slowly began to yank it back towards the creek that snaked off through a thicket of trees.

'You know I'm amazed that it even worked,' Stan said as he pulled the boat up to the creek's embankment and stepped aside.

'I told you, Stan, that you could change the environment just by thinking about it,' Lysis said, giving the boat a final nudge that sent it over the edge and splashing down into the muddy creek's river below.

Heparin, who was still seated inside the boat, clung

on to the wooden seat with outstretched claws for dear life, as the boat sprang back up, covering him in the orange and brown water.

Stan slid down the bank into the shallow water and climbed in. 'Yes, but I never thought it would work. I mean, I summoned a jet stream of water from up under the boat with such force that it sent it flying up here with ease from the oasis river. It's incredible! it truly is!' Stan said, feeling flabbergasted again.

Stan had focused his mind for what seemed like hours when he finally had the breakthrough he wanted.

The river had begun to spit and hiss, creating air pockets at the surface.

It was like the pressure of a boiling pot, that started to build under the overturned boat, when all at once the entire river seemed to get sucked up beneath the boat, leaving the fish that were once happily swimming around, now flapping and gasping on the stodgy, wet river bed.

Then with great force like a whale blowing water through its blow hole, the concentrated water thrust upwards, blasting the boat free of the basin and up over the lip, where it came to rest in the bushes above.

The water that had reached its peak, spread out like an umbrella and rained back down into the oasis, where it filtered once more into the channels. It created a river once again, to the delight of the mighty koi that were floundering and gasping.

'What's more incredible, Stan, is that you didn't smash the boat to smithereens,' Lysis said, fearful that Stan's power was stronger than he hoped it would be, for he knew the stronger the power, the more Stan was slipping from reality.

Stan held onto a tuft of grass overhanging the bank and gestured to Lysis to join him as he kept the boat steady. Lysis climbed down and positioned himself at the rear with his feet spread out around the gunwale, with his forked tail hanging over into the river.

Stan manoeuvred himself under the large body of his coffin fly companion and squirmed on the wet seating.

Heparin, who was looking bedraggled, pounced on Stan's lap and began to pad at his tuxedo.

'So how the hell do we move this craft then, Lysis?' Stan said from under the shadow of his friend's bulking form.

'Quite simple really, Stan, I will use myself as the rudder and my tail as an outboard motor. I will spin my tail in the water as a propeller to send us on our way.'

'Genius, Lysis,' Stan remarked as he gave him a thumbs-up.

Stan looked on ahead as Lysis begun to move the boat to the centre of the creek. He noticed the trees up ahead that aligned both sides of the bank, were not as green as he once remembered. It was like it was autumn, as the brown and blackened leaves fell away from the branches and delicately spun down to the river, where they created ever-decreasing circles, before they sailed away in spirals.

As the three unlikeliest of companions sailed along the river they passed beneath the overhanging trees that formed a thick canopy overhead, sheltering them from the soft glow of the eclipse high above.

Stan watched it disappear behind a rolling cloud. 'So what does the eclipse signify then, Lysis?' he said, pointing through the tangle of branches.

'It heralds a change is coming, Stan, a time of renewal,' Lysis said, as he shifted his mass left, to adjust the boat right. He felt ashamed that he was withholding more information from Stan, but figured now was not the time to share more.

Stan, lost in thought, stroked Heparin, who by now was curled up on his lap and giving off a deep purr.

'So what of my father-in-law Nathaniel? Why would he leave the sanctuary to want another chance of life? Why defy them?'

Lysis stopped spinning his tail and let the boat drift. 'I wish I knew the answer to that, Stan, but I don't. I can only presume that something has changed in him. When we finally catch up with him, then we can ask him.'

Stan nodded, with fear and trepidation beginning to take hold again.

The muddy incline of the creek's banks began to rise higher overhead and the trees began to peel away, opening the river up wider, as it funnelled out to the sea in the distance.

Stan could just make it out on the horizon, as he settled back into his seat again.

Without warning, he felt the flow of the river increasing behind them, when all of a sudden the boat lurched forward, sending him and his two fellow occupants forward.

'We've hit a snag, Stan,' Lysis shouted over the sound of the water that was building up intensity around the back of the boat.

Stan peered over the side of the boat and got his face sprayed with the gushing murky water.

He spat out the taste in disgust. 'I see it. There's a half-submerged, fallen tree jutting up from the murky depths here,' he said, using his tie to wipe away the silt from his lips.

'Can you free it?' Lysis yelled.

Stan grappled with the sunken tree, as the boat rocked violently. 'It's no use!' he shouted pulling his arms back, sodden wet.

Stan decided that if he could jettison the boat earlier with little fuss, then this would be a simple matter of...

The river began to steadily rise, the boat rising with it, unhitching it from the tree, when suddenly both sides of the muddy creek burst and poured down all around them, creating a landslide.

The boat spun round as the sliding mud crashed into the hull.

Stan was thrown back into the seat and Lysis found himself throwing his weight into the oncoming rush of mud to stop the boat upending.

The row boat spun on as the hull was battered from every angle, followed by a loud crack as a thick-set tree was uprooted from the bank and fell toward them.

At the last minute, a large wave of water mixed with the slimy mud, rose up and catapulted the boat through the air, narrowly avoiding the tree, as it crashed down at their rear.

The branches buffeted the bottom of the hull mid-flight and sent them all flying clear of the boat and out onto the waiting beach. The boat continued its flight and flipped over their heads, spinning wildly as it came crashing down in front of them.

Stan, who hit the soft sand face first, flipped onto his back and spat out mouthfuls.

Lysis, who had landed on all fours, scuttled round to face the creek as the muddy earth and roaring water torrent, carrying the trees and debris, came flooding past to meet up with the incoming tide of the sea, dying out as the two opposing forces collided.

Heparin being the lightest, had tumbled out and had ended up skidding sideways into a mound of loose stones in a rock pool, that a crab had been hiding behind, minding its own business. Now it was squashed beneath the force of the cat's impact and the shifting stones, now only a solitary pincer remained twitching, jutting skyward.

'Okay, Stan. I think it best that you give me warning next time you decide to use your power,' Lysis said.

Stan wiped the coarse sand from his face. 'Good point, Lysis,' he said, feeling somewhat relieved.

Stan looked around and spotted an island in the distance. His heart hammered in his throat.

Lysis, sensing his thoughts, interjected. 'Before we move on then, Stan, I think we are going to have to recover the boat. But more importantly, we need to fashion you a weapon,' Lysis said, catching Stan looking to the island across the sea.

'A weapon?' Stan said, looking around.

'Yes, you're going to need one if we are to cross the Ataxia Sea in one piece,' Lysis said, scanning the shoreline.

'The Ataxia Sea? Where on earth am I going to get a weapon from around here?' Stan said.

'The neck tie you're wearing, Stan, may be a good

start,' Lysis said.

Stan looked at Lysis, perplexed. He smoothed down his silk tie until his hand found the pointed end hanging above his waist. 'I don't understand,' he said.

'You will shortly, Stan, and whilst we're at it, I think we should turn your suit from a suit of fabric into one of armour too.'

Stan wrinkled his frown and gave Lysis a confused look.

He made his way to the boat that was once again upside down and sat down on the curve of the hull.

He cast a look to his tuxedo and back to Lysis. 'I have no idea what you're talking about. But okay... I'm in.'

'Essence before existence, Stan. Everything is created from a simple idea and made solid on Earth. The same principle applies here,' Lysis said, turning from the crashing waves and a speck of seaweed floating at its surface.

14

SUBARACHNOID VOID

William Last couldn't believe his luck when he had finally acquired the challis that would grant him access to paradise. He had a real chance to earn his wings and escape the confines of the prison that was Stanley Palmer's mind.

By using the winged key he possessed to combine with the vessel, he would have unlimited power to fulfil his very desire, earn his wings that were denied him so long, and set him free of this land.

But that wasn't to be. Two years ago he had been duped by Thrombus, the hideous manifestation of Stan's blood clot that had tricked him into doing her bidding. The very haemorrhage that had put Stan into his coma.

Will felt her coursing through his very being as her overwhelming deep-seeded power started to eat away at him from the inside out, changing him into her and slowly snuffing out his very existence, catching him alight in the process, creating his very own baptism of fire.

William Last, with one final act of defiance, threw himself headlong into the raging torrent of the oasis lake which acted as a centrifuge to the thalamus of Stan's brain.

He hoped that the remaining healing properties of the water that circled the oasis island, would counteract the change that was taking hold and restore his soul, in turn destroying Thrombus forever.

It was all in vain though. Thrombus had extracted Will's soul from his spirit and cast his soul out as she devoured his essence, making it whole in her reddened, bulbous image.

The lost soul of Will drifted aimlessly in the depths as he watched on helplessly to the surface, at Thrombus rising from the ashes once more. Powerless and defenceless, all he could do was look on gravely as the vessel he was attached to slowly passed from the light overhead to the darkness below.

Then his fortune changed. From above, a large muffled splash greeted his ears as two struggling figures descended into his mist.

It was Hyper, one of the Virchow's Triad whose mission was to aid Thrombus in achieving her wishes, followed by Stan himself, who was wrestling with the burnt, short Triad member.

Will watched on from the quiet depths as he saw Stan try to pry a garrotted whip from around his own neck.

Hyper's gurgling screams escaped him in air bubbles, as suddenly he caught sight of Will festooned to the challis, that once served as a communication device directly to Thalamus himself.

Free from his binds and given the upper hand, Stan pulled the whip away and used the sharp talon ends of the whip to drive into Hyper's exposed flesh before he kicked away for the surface.

Will took the rare opportunity he was given and reached out for Hyper. He drove his fused hands holding the challis into the exposed gash of Hyper, like a parasite burying into a host.

Will pushed with all his might and wriggled his way in, just as Hyper's soul was leaving his spirit behind.

As Thrombus had robbed him of his essence, so too would Will do the same of Hyper, the short, stocky, burnt, and badly scarred Triad member.

Will's devoid soul seeped into the now empty vessel of Hyper and like trying on a new suit, Will spread out his soul into the empty shell, allowing him to free the challis in the process.

After a moment to adjust in his newly acquired form, Will channelled his remaining strength to force the challis back out through the exposed wound, where upon doing so, he seized it, before it fell away.

He then proceeded to peel the winged key from its resting niche.

He discarded the cup and drifted off towards the surface with the winged key in his grasp.

Greeted by the haze of light, Will pulled himself out and onto the bank using a felled overhanging stone pillar to pull himself free.

He glanced over his shoulder, in time to see Stan holding a whip aloft, with his back to Will, jumping down into a hole at the centre of the island of the oasis.

Feeling feeble and weak, Will made for the cover of trees and hid from sight, sitting down at the base of a large oak tree.

The dainty but strikingly detailed winged key

twinkled ethereally in his hands as he spun it by both tips. Smiling inwardly, Will took the key and reached over his shoulder, placing the key between his shoulder blades.

The key like a planted seed, rooted in and began to grow, sending a sharp pain up his spine.

Will fell onto all fours in agony, as the wings took hold, immediately sprouting larger and larger from his back, casting a shadow over him.

Then they were fully formed as he flexed them in and out.

The winged key was his saviour and it had ultimately become what he had always desired; he had earned his own wings after all. The power was his now, to do whatever he wished to do with it. Revenge was high on his agenda, but one thing he had learnt from all this was to be patient and patient he was.

William Last could finally feel something that he had not felt for some time as he took the skies and soared high above the clouds – freedom to come and go where he liked.

But he knew that he would not truly be free unless he could leave this landscape of Stan's troubled mind, along with all the others that existed here.

The plasminogen was taking effect, as Stan began to get his life back. Will noticed this as he glided overhead to the changing landscape below.

Will passed through the clouds and he knew that Stan would soon be at full health, having destroyed Thrombus again. But he also knew that time was not eternal and sooner or later Stan would return, whether it be temporary or permanently; the internal scars left behind were evident.

Will knew he would need to find refuge and as he travelled on his long-distance journey to find it, it was then that he stumbled across one such place.

Leading away from the shoreline of Stan's island oasis was a submerged sand bank that could only be viewed from high above. Will followed its path through the sea, until at last he came across the towering ramparts of Petra's island far off in the distance.

It was there that he made his temporary home on the fringes of the island.

Over time he had witnessed Alcina and her companion Goliath going about their daily rituals and made every effort to stay hidden. It was also where he gleaned damning insight two years later, when his old mentor Nathaniel paid an unexpected visit to Alcina.

Nathaniel wanted reincarnation as badly as Will wanted revenge.

It was amazing to know what lengths someone would go through to achieve such things.

What better way to get revenge than to have it all for myself, Will thought.

In the bargain he would kill two birds with one stone. He would steal Nathaniel's dream and free himself of this world once more by becoming Stan's son instead of his old mentor Nathaniel.

Resentment for his old master was strong for what he did to him; his mentor deserved his fate, however unintentional.

He needed Stan, however, to witness it all, as it would be the icing on the cake to see Stan's face when he realised too late what was going to happen and would not be able to do anything about it.

But here Will was now.

THE OASIS OF FEAR

The silly woman, Petra, had tried to make him do some cheap parlour trick with a stick.

He didn't know what trick the real Goliath could do because he never had the life bond with the woman, so he had to improvise or be rumbled ahead of schedule. So far though, it had all turned out rather well. Two years of waiting, watching and planning had all led to this moment.

So where the hell is Stan? He should be here by now, Will thought.

William Last, the derived version of himself, now a manufactured subarachnoid condition of Stanley Palmer, had tired of living in the void for this long.

Now was the time to inflict a master stroke on Stan... literally.

William had many powers that he had harnessed over time, but none greater than the power to now invoke a stroke, one that would lead to the death of Stan.

The eclipse was ripe and the angel of death would soon be upon them.

Curious as to why the portal that was the eclipse to paradise was open, the dark angel would soon come for the source and think that Stan was the cause that opened it.

Will had also learnt to change his appearance into many forms and so had acquired his old image of his true self and had discarded Hyper's image forever. Now was the time to put his plans into effect; an eclipse would soon open and death would appear from within, death that would signal the end of Stan forever.

For Stan a relapse would be as good as a rest... Eternal rest!

15

SHADOW OF A FORMER SELF

Nathaniel slowly realised as he bled out into the cold dirt that if he could not have the blood of a gull to be drip fed onto his open wound, then he would soon perish.

The properties of the gull's blood would fuse with his own to create a glue-like bond and stem any further bleeding taking place. He knew he could survive, but the risk could mean that he would not be able to talk anymore.

The risk would be worth it though, as he had to make amends to Petra for his own foul doing earlier. Dying once was bad enough. But to die twice and in the astral plane too, would mean he would become a lost soul that would be damned for all eternity.

The first time he had drifted over from life felt like a long time past.

He had been at the peak of fitness by training religiously every day.

He had even entered many a tournament to prove his might, but at the expense of steroids to help him shape his massive form. His competitive nature had blinded him to the risks of drugs, as he battled to improve his physique to become the best of the best.

Then one day whilst working arduously in the gym pushing weights that far exceeded his limits, his heart failed under pressure and the life of Nathaniel Bloom was no more. He thought that was the end of his journey, but he couldn't have been farther from the truth.

There existed a spiritual world of a higher state of consciousness. One where good and evil were locked in an everlasting struggle for dominance. Nathaniel thrived here more than he did on earth, as he was not bound by the restraints of earth any longer.

He could push himself as far as he liked. Even to the point of earning his wings and progressing further still into paradise, once he had trained a guardian in the way of all things. But there was no more to achieve once he had entered through the veil. He either conformed to the tranquil ways of his creators or fought in their battles in the plain. He chose the latter, thinking that he could keep himself motivated and continue pushing his greatness by vanquishing his foes.

But over time it became stale and slowly dulled his senses.

Disillusioned and feeling hollow, he challenged his masters only to be cast out entirely.

Luckily for him, the foresight into the way of the world pathed him a way to be reborn again.

But he now realised what he had forgotten over time. How precious a life truly is and the damage and hurt that could be inflicted on others by having selfish needs and drives.

The lesson was always about caring and nurturing, to help those in need to realise their potential and greatness, thus giving them the chance of knowledge to hand down through the generations.

To think he was going to deny his grandson that birthright, by hijacking his soul and putting his only daughter through a terrible torment, now racked him with guilt. The lesson was taught.

Nathaniel rolled on to his back. 'Will, I have seen the error of my ways and so must you,' he said, clasping his hand around his neck.

Will ceased approaching a terrified Petra and turned to the fallen angel before him. 'I don't think...'

'You will not be truly free by your course of action, I see it clearly now. Love is the key, not desire,' Nathaniel said as his blood oozed between his fingers.

Will laughed hysterically. 'You know nothing of love, Nathaniel, you left me alone here to look out for Stan and look where that led. I was betrayed by them, when all I ever wanted was to have what you were promised. What you promised I would get... eventually.'

Petra looked from her dad to Will and over to the gate.

'No. I was wrong! I see that now. What I had was here all along... the love and support of my family, whom I would be reunited with over time. Not some pathetic, selfish need to have more than I truly need.'

'I can start over, have a new life... Then when I finally return here again, I can find a new host and do it all over. No longer will I be a puppet to them,' Will spat.

Petra began to back away as Will had turned his back to her.

Nathaniel forced himself to sit up. 'If you commit to this atrocity then you will rob my grandson of a life. One for him to experience for himself in all its ups and downs.' Nathaniel added, 'You must see this? You will escape one prison only to end up in another and for what? To know what you already know and not learn from it. Petra will feel inside that you are not truly her son and will come to resent you. In turn you will tear her world apart and in return you will have no life worth living for.'

'I will take my chances, Nathaniel. I can be free forever,' Will said delightedly.

Nathaniel noticed from the corner of his eye Petra vaulting the gate and out of sight. He breathed a sigh of relief.

'Like me you have become a shadow of your former self, Will. We can both start over again now. No more living in the shadows. We can embrace the light and head to paradise together, where we can accept our punishment for all of this.'

'I will never follow you again, Nathaniel. Petra is my salvation now,' Will said, turning round to face Petra, only to find her missing.

Letting out an almighty scream, on realising Petra had gone, Will ghosted into his tornado form in anger and spun across the meadow in pursuit, before smashing through the wooden picket gate and obliterating it into a thousand splinters.

Nathaniel prayed his daughter would get away safely and that sooner rather than later Stan and Lysis would show up to her aid.

Propping himself up on the mound of dirt, Nathaniel began to gather the last of his waning strength, knowing that the only thing he could do now, was to dig down into the mound and destroy the devil seed of Thrombus growing below. If not for his sake, then for the safe wellbeing of his daughter in the real world.

Night was descending, but the stars were dying out.

This last act of redemption he hoped would be his only light.

16

THE ATAXIA SEA

A mist had settled on the calm sea and night had fallen.

The eclipse had separated, leaving a waning moon behind and the sun had vanished from view. The only light from the moon now, to guide the occupants of the little row boat across the large body of water.

Stan was huddled in the boat with Heparin on his lap and Lysis again was at the rear, steering them through the blanketing silence.

Stan thrust his right hand skyward and admired the glint from the tip of the sword, that extended from the attachment on his arm.

Earlier with Lysis' help, Stan had loosened his tie from his neck and as instructed by his friend, wrapped one end of it around his wrist, leaving the large pointed end hanging loose across the back of his hand. Lysis promised him that it would serve two purposes. One to fight and one as a reminder that when he finally awoke, it would prompt memories of what had occurred here.

With great concentration and focus, Stan had solidified the neck tie into that of hard steel, which now extended from the wrist band he had created, by mind control alone.

After marvelling at his newfound power, he had turned his attention to his suit and had easily morphed it from fabric into hard leather armour, but that it still retained the same shape in the process. Empowering him, it gave Stan a new zest of life for the battle that lay ahead.

But as he stared through the mist to his wife's lonely island in the distance, dread began to take hold.

'I fear I'm going to lose Petra and my son,' Stan said, looking up to Lysis.

Lysis stopped swishing his tail in the pitch-black sea and let the boat drift. 'You've been through so much, Stan, and it's only fair to say, your mind has ruled your heart of late. You can be forgiven for the way you have been. It's not your fault that your worsening condition has made you have a short temper. I'm sure Petra understands this better than anyone.'

'It's not just that though, is it, Lysis? If we don't succeed, then how do I cope without them? I won't be able to forgive myself.'

Lysis lifted a sticky foot and touched Stan's shoulder for reassurance. 'I'm sure we will win out in the end, Stan. The bigger issue is, how will they cope without you when the time comes?'

'If my fate is signed, sealed and delivered, then yes. I just hope that I can make things right with Petra and give my son the right start to life. That's all I can do, right? After all, that's what we exist for, isn't it?' Stan said, stroking a deeply purring Heparin on his lap. 'Looks like I was doomed to fail,' he added glumly.

Lysis was just about to answer, when something hit the side of the boat with a loud thud.

Heparin awoke with a start and his ears pricked back in alarm. He scrabbled from Stan's lap and jumped onto the bow where he peered over into the dark abyss and began to make a low, eerie whine.

Stan grabbed the side of the boat to get a better look, then cast his eye to Lysis. 'What the hell was that?' he said, feeling spooked.

'I was feeling optimistic that we might be left alone, but it would seem that we are in more danger than I fear, Stan,' Lysis said, removing his tail from the water and curling it into the boat.

Stan reached out and scooped up Heparin to his chest, trying to console him. 'What does that mean?' he said, looking around nervously, whilst trying to soothe the cat.

'It means that you should ready your sword.'

'For what?'

'The seaweed, Stan!' Lysis remarked.

Stan gave an uncertain look, when more thudding from the underside of the hull caused the boat to rock violently.

'The oasis is your thalamus, to which you know I am bonded, and the island is your mind. The seaweed that lies beneath the Ataxia Sea are representative of the nerves that attach to your spinal cord in life, Stan, without them your island would not exist, but they shouldn't cause us any concern...' Lysis pondered momentarily. 'Unless...?! I've changed my mind. We HAVE to get to Petra's island with haste, Stan, and whatever you do, DON'T SEVER THE SEAWEED!' Lysis bellowed, hoping that he had got it wrong. '...If I'm right, then things are much more worse than I feared.'

Lysis dipped his tail back into the sea and spun it rapidly.

The boat lurched forward and they were off again cutting through the still sea and the mist.

Stan rose to his feet and peered at Petra's fortress. 'We're almost there, Lysis, but we have to be careful of the rocks,' he said, turning back to his friend.

Lysis went to smile, when something snagged around his tail; he knew only too late what it was.

A tendril snaked around his tail and yanked him, squealing, free from the boat, pulling him below the surface as he thrashed blindly.

Stan's face turned to horror. 'Lysis!' he screamed.

He was met with silence, as the sea settled once more, leaving he and Heparin alone and vulnerable, bobbing aimlessly to and fro.

Stan lunged for the boat's stern to find Lysis, but he was met with a branching tendril of seaweed that broke through the surface, making him reel in surprise, forcing him onto his back. With more sprays of water, tendrils from all directions shot out toward the boat and slung themselves over the edges of the vessel on all sides, with sickeningly wet splodges.

Heparin arched his back and puffed himself out, hissing at the tendrils, as they slithered towards him.

Stan quickly recovered and began to slice at the silent attackers, dicing and slicing at the tube-like structures that emitted a foul stench of oozing water from within with each slice.

With every tendril that Stan cut away though,

another quickly replaced it, leaving an exhausted Stan helpless.

Then came through the surface a dome, made of interconnecting seaweed that formed a mesh-like pattern that dwarfed the size of the boat and almost capsized it. At its centre, all tangled up, was Lysis, who began to spew water from his mouth as he struggled to suck in oxygen now he had been raised above the surface.

'Lysis, are you okay?' Stan shouted.

Lysis struggled against his bonds, but the seaweed only tightened around him firmer. 'I think so, Stan,' he gasped. 'Just don't do any anything rash,' he added.

Stan's mind raced. *There has to be something I can do, something here I can do with my power,* he thought.

An idea began to form for Stan, when over the side of the gunwale, a pair of slimy hands crept into view, followed by another to his left and another pair to his right.

Stan backed away and slid unceremoniously on the fresh carpet of seaweed that now covered the floor of the hull. He fell hard onto his backside and almost toppled over the other side when another pair of hands caught him from behind, pinning him down.

Then four faces appeared. Faces of children that looked dank, slimy, grey and rotten.

Drowned corpses that pulled themselves up and into the boat, joining a terrified Stan and a skittish Heparin.

Stan found himself retching as he began to vomit.

The vision came back to Stan. Their terrified faces when the minibus plunged down the ravine. The children who were with him but were not so lucky, drowned or had passed away on impact.

These were the slightly familiar faces of his fallen classmates. Now lifeless and soulless, lost to limbo for eternity, to be damned for their tragic fates.

Stan, overcome with grief, burst into tears. 'I could not help you, I was young, I was scared... it was horrible,' he blurted.

'Fffrrreee usss!' they all whispered in unison.

'Join usss, Ssstan!' they wailed.

Lysis wriggled. 'Don't listen to them, Stan, they will damn you too.'

Tears were streaming down Stan's cheeks, as he looked pleadingly to the children. 'I, I can't help you. I don't know how. I'm sorry...' he said, trying to back away.

One of the children turned away from him, a little girl.

Stan remembered her name. 'Grace, I'm sorry, I couldn't reach you in time,' Stan said sniffling as he reached out to her.

Then he noticed she was tethered by her spine to the seaweed. He followed its trail as it snaked away and out from sight over the lip of the boat to connect to the floating dome.

Another child, a boy this time. Stan knew him as Adron, grabbed hold of Stan's wrist with the sword attached and swung it feebly up and down. 'Fffrrreee usss,' he said.

Stan realised then what he must do, as he noticed that all the children were tethered to the dome.

Lysis sensed what was coming. 'No, Stan, you can't! If you free them, then you will damn yourself, your oasis, your island, will fall... your lifespan will diminish greatly.'

Stan looked to Lysis, sobbing. 'But I have to, Lysis, they're just children.'

'But it's not your fault, Stan,' Lysis said, just before a tendril wrapped around his head and quietened him.

All four children had now turned their backs on Stan, exposing their leashes, leaving Stan in the centre.

'I'm sorry, Lysis, but I have to. It was my fault we crashed!' Stan said with his eyes glazing over. 'I had stashed my comic away after reading it into the pouch on the back seat in front of me. Adron snatched it up to read and I got mad with him, so I shouted at him. The driver was distracted just for a second and that was all it took. If I hadn't shouted, then maybe they would still be alive.'

Lysis slumped against his reins in defeat.

Stan steeled himself and hacked at the exposed tendrils on the children's backs; in an instance the deed was done.

'Please forgive me,' Stan wailed as he fell to his knees.

The hollow children smiled at him and one by one they faded from view as they slipped back overboard to sink back into the dark Ataxia Sea.

The tendrils that held the boat steadfast slunk back over the lip and splashed noisily into the sea, and the dome that held Lysis captive began to disintegrate. He fell from its grasp heavily into the cold depths of the Ataxia Sea once more, screaming for Stan to rescue him.

Stan, having regained some of his senses, leant over and hauled the giant coffin fly back on board, where they both collapsed in a heap, sighing.

A new noise hit Stan's ears though, as in the corner of the boat was Heparin choking on what Stan could only think was a fur ball.

'What now?' he said.

But he did not have the chance to check on the cat, as a deafening crack signalled behind them.

Sitting bolt upright, Stan looked back to his island. 'What on earth is that?'

Lysis swivelled back round and said gravely, 'The death of my home and your second chance.'

The island had ruptured across its middle where the oasis once nestled, and the waterfalls were now spewing water from the sea into its very basin. Rivers overflowed and the trees in the valley of lost souls were buried beneath the collapse of the high mountaintop's rubble.

Lysis peeled his one good eye away from the devastating scene before him and climbed back into position on the boat. 'We should concentrate on the journey ahead now, Stan. There is nothing back there for us anymore.'

Stan tried to find some comforting words for his friend as to why he did what he had done, but he figured it was best left alone.

Picking up a heaving Heparin, Stan tried to soothe the cat's neck and he became more worried by the minute. 'What's wrong with him, Lysis?' he said.

Another loud crack and a large rumble behind them signalled the last fight of the island giving into the sea, as it sank spectacularly from view, just leaving the peaks of the mountains on show, as it sent out large tidal waves in its wake.

'No time to explain, Stan, we are about to have company,' Lysis said, concerned on seeing the giant waves rushing their way.

The waves roared in velocity as they chased the tiny speck of the boat enveloped in the mist, creating a vacuum that dispersed the mist before it.

Stan laid Heparin down and craned his neck for a better look, just as the wind sailed through, blowing the mist away.

'I can see a little better now the mist has gone, but I can't see the horizon,' Stan shouted.

Then Stan looked higher and saw just how much jeopardy they were truly in, as the tidal waves loomed high in the night sky.

'Stan. We are either going to drown or we are going to end up being smashed to smithereens on Petra's island, so I suggest you think of something quickly.'

Stan, still not fully recovered from his ordeal, wracked his mind trying to decide what to do.

'I'm serious, Stan, we don't have a lot of time!' Lysis screamed as his tail spun on overtime below the surface.

'Turn and face it, I've got an idea,' Stan said, sounding not overconfident at all.

Lysis shot him a concerned look, but did as requested, as he shifted his weight and brought the boat round in an ark.

'I hope you know what you're doing, Stan!' he said, alarmed.

Stan couldn't hear Lysis over the deafening roar and just gave an 'OK' signal with his hand before plunging it into the sea, closing his eyes.

Then the wave was upon them.

The power that Lysis had generated from his tail had taken the boat halfway up the wall of the tidal wave, but he knew that was all he had and soon the wave would topple them and churn them up like butter.

He braced himself and bowed his head to imminent death.

But to Lysis' astonishment it never happened. The sound of the roaring waves was replaced by a crackling sound. Instead the whole sea, including the giant waves, had frozen solid; somehow Stan had iced them over.

Stan removed his cold hand and placed it under his armpit. 'Phew, that was a close one,' he said, feeling relieved.

Lysis raised his head and looked around. Sure enough, Stan had delivered and here they were, now suspended halfway up a frozen wall embedded into its mountainous icy face.

'Now all I have to do is give a little heat to the boat and we can sled this boat onwards to the island,' Stan said, feeling quite proud of himself.

Lysis was about to protest, when all of a sudden the boat broke free of its unworldly mooring and began its icy descent.

Lysis hankered down into the boat just in time and flattened Stan and Heparin beneath him.

The boat tipped onto its side and almost threw the occupants out as it made its rapid journey towards the island.

'So, do you have a plan to stop this ride then, Stan?' Lysis hollered.

Stan didn't get a chance to answer, as the boat hit the rocks of the island with such speed that it was cleaved in two, ejecting all three members of its cargo once more.

By the time Stan and Lysis had recovered they realised that Heparin was missing.

All that remained of his whereabouts were paw prints leading away from beyond the rock's sand strip, off to a chiselled-out stairway set into a high cliff.

To Stan and Lysis' puzzlement, the paw prints had changed with every step. The prints remained the same but they had grown in size with each imprint, getting larger and more deep-set within the sand.

The journey had just taken a more unexpected turn and one in a place that was alien to them.

The dread inside them was mounting; only once before had Stan felt so scared, but this was new.

The unknown of Petra's oasis, her oasis of hope now dripped in fear.

17

THE CAT'S MEOW

Dustin entered through the back door, whistling, with a garden spade swinging in his hand, and propped it against the kitchen cupboard.

Natasha approached him and gave him a funny look as she passed him a steaming hot cup of tea. 'Thank you for doing this,' she said, planting a kiss on his cheek.

'Yeah, sure. Anything I can do to help you out,' Dustin said, before he blew across the tea to cool it down.

Natasha strode past him and hung out the door looking into the rear garden.

It was a cold, frosty evening and the mildew clung onto the short grass that made up the narrow lawn. A small plot of freshly dug earth lay, offset in the right far corner, where a raised flower bed had been freshly disturbed. Surrounded on all sides by creeping wintergreen lay a deep hole that had been carefully shaped into a foot-long rectangle.

'Is it deep enough, babe?' Natasha said, pulling her cardigan tight around her chest.

'I hope so,' Dustin said, as he proceeded to slurp

his tea.

'Okay well I think it's time then,' Natasha said, as she turned in from the cold and made her way back through the kitchen to the hallway.

To the left of the hallway lay the entrance to the living room, where seated inside on a large cream leather sofa, sat Anastasia beside her younger sister Sally.

The sisters were hugging each other and were distraught with grief. Both had tears streaming down their eyes, as between them rested a large shoebox with a peaceful Heparin the cat curled up inside.

Natasha made her way over to them and reached inside the box, giving a tender stroke along the length of the cat's body.

'I'm sure your mum and dad would be proud of you girls,' she said, as she saw what they had put in the box with Heparin.

A family photo had been placed between Heparin's legs, along with his favourite toy mouse and his sparkly collar.

Natasha turned from the girls and retrieved the lid to the shoe box from the glass coffee table. 'We are ready now girls, if you are?' she said fondly.

Anastasia looked to Sally and nodded.

Sally picked up the box carefully and hugged it close to her as Anastasia put an arm around her shoulder and ushered her from the room.

Led by Natasha, the two girls followed behind and passed by Dustin, who bowed his head and swiftly retrieved his spade.

Then the procession was off, crunching over the

frost hardened grass.

Sally approached the grave and placed the box gently within, whilst trying to fight back more tears. Anastasia took the lid from Natasha and placed it gently over the box.

'Would you like to say something, girls?' Natasha said, as she put an arm around Dustin for warmth.

Sally couldn't hold back the tears any longer and just stood there sobbing, shaking her head.

'I would like to say a few words,' Anastasia said, as she wiped the tears from her sister's face. 'Thank you, Heparin for bringing us all so much joy and for the cosy warm cuddles, when you could be bothered,' she half laughed. 'We will miss you and will cherish all the fond memories you gave us,' she added before sobbing uncontrollably.

Natasha found herself crying too, as she nuzzled into Dustin's oversized sweater. 'Rest in peace,' she sniffed.

*

Heparin having been ejected clear of the boat once more, had fared better than his crewmates. He had landed upright on all fours, but something felt different within him.

As he stood there taking in this new unexplored world, the choking feeling was getting worse within his throat.

He opened his mouth wide and forced the blockage he could feel to the surface, by a gagging. Within moments, a ball of long sinewy matted hair came forth and fell onto the sand.

Guiltily he pawed sand over it, to hide it from view, then trotted off, feeling much better.

But then with his super keen hearing, he heard a far-off voice coming from everywhere all at once. It belonged to the large human female, who had played with him when he was alive.

He couldn't understand her words but they were soothing and filled him with a harmony that he did not know he had.

Then he felt himself changing as he walked along with every step. He felt himself getting stronger.

He let out a long meow in gratitude, then another that sounded to him more like a roar!

*

'Did you hear that?' Sally said.

'Yes, I did!' exclaimed Anastasia.

The sisters both smiled at each other and hugged.

'What did you hear?' Natasha said, looking to the girls and to Dustin for clarification. Dustin just shrugged.

'A meow! Heparin gave us a meow!' the sisters said together.

'I didn't hear anything,' Natasha said. *But if it gives you both comfort, then it is all right with me,* she thought.

*

Heparin swiped his tongue across his fangs. Something had certainly changed within him, for that he was sure. Even his paws looked bigger and his colouring had changed.

Unbeknown to him, however, was just how much of a transition had taken place. The newly formed leopard that was Heparin, sauntered off and made his way to the large steps cut into the cliff in the distance.

18

KINDRED SPIRITS

Whilst the earlier eclipse had been aligned perfectly, a large dark angel had slipped through its outer rim unseen.

As it beat its mighty wings across the astral plane's skies, it looked back to the distance and watched the eclipse separate, heralding the closure of the doorway between the astral plane and paradise.

When it was satisfied that the danger in the plain was no longer a threat, it would open the seal once more and return.

Its large black wings were comprised of razor-sharp individual feathers that criss-crossed one another, creating multiple scissor-like actions, as the wings flexed back and forth.

In the dark angel's claw-like hands, it wielded a long weapon in the shape of a spike.

Its face was hidden by a long, hooded black cloak that flapped noisily in the breeze, as it scoured the landscape below.

From its aerial view it could see all the various islands for miles around. Some large and some small, some grand and majestic, whilst others looked plain and pitiful.

There were interconnecting islands and some separated by the seas that surrounded them, that maybe should not be.

There were also newly forming islands that signalled new life of birth on Earth. Again, some were anchored to larger islands and some were lonely mounds of dirt, abandoned on their own.

The dark angel felt more sorry for these islands than most.

As it looked down upon the islands, it could also make out some that had once been, now barely visible beneath the ocean of tranquillity, the Ataxia.

Each island was like a single solar system that existed in a larger galaxy and all fanned out from one central point in space – a large continental island, where an eternal war was being waged for supremacy between the evil and the pure.

It sensed the tide of battle was being turned in their favour, as for every ally that sacrificed itself, another was ready to take up arms.

With every 55 million humans that died every year, there were over 131 million more born, ready to carry on the mantle. But it was the 55 million that were the most important in the war, as their numbers were declining, as man found ever more elaborate ways to prolong life and so, there laid the problem.

The quest for eternal life on Earth was harming nature's very existence and survival.

Of the few souls that passed over successfully, some were already evil in nature to their core and some were turned to those ways, whilst some were lost forever.

The playing field was becoming less even and a state of stalemate would soon be broken. Because of the increase in births, souls that had expired were now having to share islands to cope with the influx of overpopulation; that too, was just as harmful to the natural balance of things.

This was where souls were more vulnerable, as their whereabouts could not be monitored quite so easily, therefore they were susceptible to being taken against their will for the role of evil.

But this was inconsequential to the dark angel, as the eclipse had not been its doing but that of an individual's arrival to the plain that was now harnessing a great power.

Something on this scale had not been witnessed for a millennium.

The dark angel's mission was to prevent evil flowing through to paradise, by shutting down the catalyst for the eclipse creation.

It could feel the great power of this being and knew that it had escaped the confines of its island and was now putting another island in jeopardy.

The dark angel knew that its masters must know of the reasoning behind this temporal manifestation. But as they never shared their insights, the dark angel felt the duty of care was its own to investigate further.

It dropped in altitude and soared for the battle-strewn island where it took in the magnitude of the bloody carnage that was taking place.

Shrouded by the darkening sky it eyed the vista below.

A small group of white-winged angels sensed the dark angel's arrival and broke free from their pact.

They formed a tightknit formation and streaked upwards like a flock of angry birds, scattering loose feathers to the four corners of the winds.

The dark angel nodded curtly to the five angels that greeted it. 'Follow,' it said.

The small group of angels knew better than to disobey and fell in to formation behind it, sharing worried glances with one another. They could scarcely believe the angel of death was here and now.

Some thought that it was merely a fable, others believed it a legend to keep up morale. But this, they now knew was only too real.

With magnificent speed the angels passed away from the battle and found themselves passing by a recently semi-submerged island that they could see had been severed in two, beneath the surface of the sea.

Up ahead they noticed the ocean was not moving but had fully iced over in form with large waves looking like large icebergs.

The dark angel sensed their fears. 'Answers later, we seek the fallen.'

They circled the island and with a command of, 'Reveal,' by the angel of death, the oasis belonging to Petra appeared before them with Nathaniel at its centre, barely clinging on to his soul.

The white angels touched down in a large circular formation around him and took up a kneeled stance, readying themselves for a possible attack.

The dark angel, seeing the condition of Nathaniel, circled the sky and caught sight of a seagull that was trying to retrieve a fish frozen at the surface of the sea below.

With lightning reflexes the angel thrust its spike, which skewered the seagull, ending its life with one swift stroke.

The angel of death then returned to the oasis and gracefully flitted down to Nathaniel's side, where it slid the seagull from the spike to his feet.

Nathaniel, thinking he was delirious through lack of blood, looked nervously to the threatening sight of the dark figure before him and then to the angels that circled him.

'Are you here to claim my soul, Ictus?' Nathaniel said feebly.

'No! Drain the corpse,' the dark figure said, pointing at the seagull with a bony finger.

Nathaniel gingerly scooped up the dead gull with both hands and wrung out its blood, to drip onto his open wound around his throat, twisting the bird in opposing directions until the bird was bled dry and every drop was used. The gull's blood, on contact with his own began to sizzle and hiss, as it began to congeal, closing up the severed wound.

'I need answers from you, as to what led to this,' Ictus, the dark angel said, once it was satisfied that Nathaniel was out of the worst.

Nathaniel gave a nervous look.

'I should take you back to answer for your sins, but we are not interested in you. You have seen the error of your ways, you will make your own amends. Now talk,' it demanded.

Nathaniel looked to the grave with a now flowering black rose rooted at its mound and then back to the menacing angel before him. 'Yes, of course I will. But first... Alcina is buried here and she is changing into Thrombus,' he said solemnly. 'Please, I can't let that happen... It was my fault,' Nathaniel added, hanging his head in shame.

'Thrombus is not my concern. She will always turn up to wreak havoc. She can manifest in many forms and in many places at once. I will not waste time with matters so trivial, I demand answers of a greater concern,' Ictus demanded again, but more forcefully this time. 'Or you will feel my wrath.'

Nathaniel stood up shakily. 'Please, let me dispense with this matter and I will give you the answers you seek,' he said, holding out a hand for the pike.

Ictus brought its sharp-tipped wings up over its shoulders at such alarming speed that Nathaniel stumbled backwards onto the mound to avoid their tips, flattening the rose in the process.

Then the angel of death brought up its long spike with such ferocity that Nathaniel shielded his eyes with his hands for fear of seeing it pierce him.

But it never happened. When he finally pulled away his hands and looked again, he saw that the angel had speared the mound between his legs.

With a follow-up second jab with a twist, the spike found its mark deep beneath the soil to the pulsating beating heart of Thrombus, to end her growth.

What followed was a deep-rooted, high-pitch scream from under the mound, followed by a deathly silence.

Ictus pulled the spike clear and flicked off the blood. 'Now one last time, Nathaniel, talk?' it said, leaving Nathaniel watching the black rose beginning to wither and die.

19

CRY OF THE SOUL BIRDS

Petra didn't know how long the nightmare would last, but all she could think of was to get as far away as possible.

Problem was, she figured, sooner or later Will would catch her up and all the time she had borrowed would be for nothing.

She had an overwhelming, aching feeling in the pit of her stomach, to head down to her son's island and scoop him up, promising him that all would be safe, now that she was here to look after him. But she knew that it would probably just make matters worse and put him in even greater danger.

So, in her panicked state, she had bypassed a set of large stone steps that she presumed would lead to the foot of her island to take her to her son's island and instead headed for the rickety bridge once more. If she could make it across, then she knew another path existed that would take her through a narrow gorge that she had witnessed earlier.

Petra didn't know where the path led or what was on the other side, but she had to buy herself more time to think.

True to her dad's words, there had indeed been a large woven-net bag, containing shrieking gulls, abandoned by the side of the bridge. But having acquired the bag with its noisy, flapping birds, she now didn't know what to do with it, as she dragged it struggling behind her over the swinging bridge.

She felt sorrow for her dad, but only because she had no notion of what this world's secrets could reveal.

He thought he had found a way back home but it had come with a great cost. One that now, he was paying for, but he was still her father and she knew that she would always forgive him eventually.

If returning these scuffling birds was a way to save his soul, then it was a daughter's duty to try.

But the how, was beyond her grasp at the moment.

Gripping on to the rope railing with one hand and dragging the net in the other, she made her way across steadily.

The wind was still relentless and all she wanted to do was be reunited with Stan and the girls once more.

She battled on, hoping that this all would fade to a distant memory when she finally awoke.

Having made her way across safely and without any sign of the treacherous Will, Petra picked up the path to the gorge and paused once she had approached its entrance.

She rested her back against one side of its hulking rocky edifice and set the bag down to get her breath back.

She thought she could murder a cigarette right about now.

Looking up the path, Petra could see a plateau of rolling fields of rapeseed in the distance.

The tall bright yellow vegetation, clouded by the soft hue of night, was more than substantial to hide her away from prey.

The landscape's stark, vibrant contrast of softness, showing off her inner feminine side, as opposed to the hard rock-faceted contours she showed to the world on the other side of her island, that she had now left well and truly behind.

A maelstrom of flying debris of planks alerted her gaze.

Back across to the bridge, she spotted a mini whirlwind churning up the planks of the bridge's base, spewing them into the air to be whipped away to the sea below, as the astral form of Will made his vengeful way across.

Petra stifled a scream and snatched up the bag before hastily setting off once more on her journey into the unknown.

*

Heparin, the now transformed leopard, had been enjoying his new surroundings, when he had come across a large pool that lay before him.

He approached its murky surface and went to drink from its cool depths, when an image in its mirror-like surface, stared back at him, startling him.

The image was of a big cat with large teeth and an elongated face.

Heparin jumped back in fright, turned his ears forward and arched his back to make himself look bigger.

He approached the water once again, with more due care and attention this time, but again the big cat stared back at him.

He swiped at the surface with his large paws, creating a large ripple, and fled in the opposite direction to a path that led between a high chasm.

He had soon forgotten about the strange creature from the watering hole though, as before him the landscape opened up into tall fields mixed with the sounds of squawking birds.

His attention soon turned to locating the noisy source, because that racket, usually signalled fun.

*

Petra dragged the net further into the heart of one of the many strong-scented fields and released it from her grasp. The birds contained within the net slowly became quiet as if they too sensed something evil on the horizon.

Feeling exhausted and fearful for the crying birds giving her location away, she crawled off further into the expanse, whereon hoping she had gained enough distance, she collapsed into a heap and waited with bated breath.

Heparin, who had been silently tracking the sound of the gulls, listened intently as the cries faded away and decided to approach the last known whereabouts of the source for a sneaky surprise attack.

Then a new noise erupted far behind, as a small tornado danced this way and that, as it mowed an irregular path through the fields, sending rapeseed flying into the night sky.

Heparin didn't give this new commotion a second thought though, as by this point, he had pounced out on the unsuspecting birds and began to rip through the net with a frenzied playful burst, sending them into a lather.

The birds began to peck at their attacker, which just spurred Heparin on to free them, to have more fun, as they cried deafening wails.

The swirling devastation that was Will, heard the noise erupt and he changed his trajectory to hone in on the wailing birds, weaving his way towards them.

Having gnawed through the net, Heparin tried to seize one of the gulls, not to eat, just to play with.

But in an eruption, they all came flying out at once and made him tumble backwards just as the swirling mass made an appearance.

The cry of the soul birds rose up into the eye of the vortex as they beat their wings to try and free themselves of this new prison that they had found themselves in, as they struggled to streak up its funnel to the clear sky above.

Petra, having witnessed the scene unfold, rose to her feet and made a run for it.

Heparin, who was as equally alarmed as the gulls, bolted off and caught sight of Petra doing the same as what he had in mind in the distance.

He raced after her as the whirlwind, unsure of what to do next, hesitated.

Petra, in a blind panic headed back for the gorge, pursued by Heparin and the now advancing seagull-infested, whirling mass of air.

The leopard caught up with Petra and tried its best to protect her. But she seemed ungrateful as she screamed at him in her strange voice, trying to wave him off.

The vortex was quicker though, as it blindsided the leopard and snatched it up into its abyss, along with the hapless Petra in its wake.

As it carried them all back off across the great expanse where the bridge once was and onto the oasis beyond, the seagulls, Heparin and Petra were all tossed around in a torrent of feathers, fur and sweat.

*

The five angels that stood poised at the oasis, heard the cries of the gulls and readied their stance. Fanning out a wall of touching wings in their circle to stop any advancing threat, they looked to the skies.

Will was not at all surprised that there would be a boarding party waiting for him, as he broke through the high conifers, splitting some of them in two.

He flung the leopard from his wake into one of the angels, sending angel and beast headlong into another nearby angel.

He then released the gulls at another, whose beaks impaled the angel to a nearby conifer, ending his and the birds' existence.

Will then picked the last two up with one swift stroke, stripping them of flesh and wings that spattered a high spinning, Petra who was helpless in the core.

Then Petra fell hard onto the mound surrounded by daisies, as Will shifted once again into his canine form.

The gigantic dog then attacked one of the angels that was trying to get back on his feet and snapped his neck between his jaws, before tossing him into an advancing angel to the right.

The last angel ruffled her feathers and sidled up

for a kill, confident that she would not be fooled again.

Will though, was one step ahead as he shifted form once more into a black liquid state that sprayed across her, causing her to slip and slide. Then having coated her fully, he oozed into her astonished open mouth and solidified himself from within, choking her of air, which ended her existence.

Once the deed was done he transformed from within her and burst forth into his twisted spectral form, exploding her into a shower of blood and feathers.

Petra lay winded and dazed on the mound, as Will strode over to her.

Heparin seized the moment and stepped between the two of them. He raised his hind quarters and lowered his front ready to spring into action.

He thwacked his tail across the ground and bared his teeth at Will, who in turn morphed back into the form of Goliath, the gigantic Tibetan mastiff.

Cat and dog squared off to one another for the ultimate showdown, leaving a petrified Petra, breathless behind them.

20

ELEVENTH HOUR

Stan gazed up at the winding stone steps to the cliff's peak and saw what remained of the sandy paw prints that were left behind.

'Lysis, I don't understand why Heparin's paw prints have changed,' he exclaimed.

Lysis scuttled over the sand dragging his large tail behind him and eyed the steps. 'It means that Heparin has been laid to rest and that he has finally transformed into his true self,' he stated.

Stan went to mount the steps. 'What true self is that?' he asked.

Lysis turned from the steps and looked around the craggy face of the sheer rock. 'That, I do not know, Stan. Come, we are not going to follow. There is something else I need you to see first,' Lysis said.

Stan looked to the giant coffin fly, perplexed, but curiosity had taken hold, as he dutifully followed.

The pair passed around the sheer slope, following the coastline, and Stan looked out to the frozen sea.

The sea had not quite frozen up to Petra's island though. It was as though the warmth of the island was keeping it at bay, creating an invisible water barrier as it lapped gracefully at the shoreline.

As they rounded the bend, Lysis looked up to the overhanging cliff face and noticed a dull orange glare radiating from over its peak.

Stan navigated through a clump of large beached rocks and caught his companion's eyeline.

'What is that up there?' he said, pointing.

'It would seem a beacon of fire was lit. I can only presume that it was created to guide Nathaniel here from your island,' Lysis said, as he continued on his way.

Stan gave one last look and hurried to catch Lysis up.

As the pair completed their walk around the broken shoreline, Stan saw a sand bank connecting from the beach to a small island in the distance.

'Is that...?'

'...Yes, Stan. The island of your unborn son!' Lysis said with trepidation in his voice.

Stan beamed a large smile. 'Am I going to see my son?' he said jubilantly.

'Yes, Stan, but be careful! Look closely... Do you see what I can see?' Lysis said, flicking up sand with his tail, as he brought it up over his back as if on guard.

Stan peered through the darkness and could just make out two shapes on the island. One sitting down like a sentry on duty, watching the coastline for threats, and another hunched over the centre of the island itself.

Before Stan had the chance to answer, the figure that had been crouching, suddenly rose to its feet as if alerted and begun to make its way towards the path of the sand bank that cut through the calm sea.

Stan readied his sword and with a curt nod from Lysis began to head towards the approaching figure.

As Stan and Lysis made their way across the narrow sand strip, Stan's footsteps became stodgy as his feet sank beneath the wet sand. Lysis though, didn't seem to have the same issue, as his padded feet didn't displace the sand.

The large brutish figure became more pronounced as Stan let out a gasp. 'So it is true then? Nathaniel... my father-in-law. The person that I looked up to and admired, here and now. The traitor that would put his daughter and grandson in danger for wanting a new life!' he said, bringing up his sword.

Nathaniel inched away with his hands in the air. 'I'm sorry, Stan, I truly am,' he said quietly.

'I SWEAR, if you've harmed them... I'll end you right here and now!' Stan said as he inched closer.

'ENOUGH!' came a piercing roar from the island.

Lysis looked startled, but realised instantly who the voice belonged to. He shot out a paw to Stan's extended weapon and retracted it back. 'It's okay, Stan, lower your weapon,' he said, swinging around to face him.

'We don't have much time, please follow me,' Nathaniel said, as he turned and made his way back for the island.

Lysis gazed upon Stan. 'It's okay, Stan,' he said, resting a pad on Stan's shoulder. 'I think I know what's happened... Come,' he added, as he turned and followed suit.

Stan loosened his gritted teeth and cautiously

looked around, before trailing after them.

Nearing the island, Stan now made out the contours of the other figure. It was a huge, black-clad, hooded angel with large black wings, comprised of sharp pointed feathers.

Its face was obscured by the hood as it sat hunched at the centre of the island.

The wings it possessed were fanned out all around it, like a hen ruffled up over a nest. It spoke. 'I am Ictus. I am curious to make your acquaintance, Stanley Palmer,' it said harshly.

Beneath it was a faint *dah dum, dah dum...* that repeated over and over.

'Tell them the story that you told me,' the dark angel said, throwing Stan off kilter.

Nathaniel massaged the wound at his throat as he struggled to find the right words to explain the past events.

Dah dum, dah dum, dah dum...

When Nathaniel was finished, he merely looked at Stan with sorrow and regret.

Dah dum...

'So where the HELL is Petra now? You said she escaped, but you don't know where? Why have you not gone searching for her?' Stan said worriedly, as he paced backwards and forwards.

Dah dum, dah dum...

'She will be quite safe, Stan. William Last will not hurt her, as he needs her soul to pass back over into your realm. There are only two places where he can achieve such a fate... Petra's oasis where my brothers are waiting, and here at your son's early formed island, where we await. So you see, we have the matter in hand. He does not stand a chance there or here,' the dark angel said confidently.

Dah dum, dah dum...

Stan couldn't focus on what was being said to him for the beating sound was silently driving him insane.

Lysis scuttled over to Ictus. 'But I'm afraid you're wrong! I think I know who opened the eclipse to bring you here as I have figured out exactly what danger we all face. I only just worked it out when Stan and I came here across the sea and encountered the children.'

Dah dum, dah dum...

'THAT'S IT! I've had enough now! I need to see,' Stan said, cutting Lysis off as he approached the nestled angel.

The angel of death sensed Stan's wishes and raised a wing. 'Of course, Stan. Please look. But I implore you, do not touch as your son is very fragile in this state,' it said, shifting its frame for Stan to get a better look.

Dah dum, dah dum, dah dum...

Stan peered beneath the dark angel and sank to his knees as he wept.

There surrounded in a fluid like sac in a submerged pool of water was his unborn son, not quite fully developed but distinguishable by his shape and mass with blackened pupils.

Dah dum, DAH DUM, DAH DUM... The beat of its heart quickened on seeing its father, getting louder in Stan's ears.

Stan wiped his tears away and looked upon his son

fondly, resisting the urge to hug him.

'Oh my god, what's that tube attached to the sac that snakes away into the depths?' Stan wailed.

'That is the umbilical cord that feeds your son's unconscious state, like the one that gives it nutrients in your world, Stan. It is nothing to be afraid of,' Ictus said, as he grabbed hold of Stan's arm, which shot a cold chill along it.

'But it's like the seaweed we encountered earlier,' Stan said to Lysis as he too came round to look.

'Yes, Stan, that is correct. That's what feeds a soul existence like yours did...' Lysis trailed off, knowing that Stan would not want reminding of his doom.

Stan stood back up and brushed the sand from his palms as the dark angel covered over his son with protection once more. 'So what were you saying before, Lysis?'

'A tulpa. Stan has created a tulpa!' Lysis said with fear.

'What on earth is a tulpa?' Stan said, bewildered.

Ictus bristled its feathers. 'That's impossible! No one has ever attempted it successfully before, let alone unwittingly.'

'Nonetheless, it explains why Will is so powerful and why he survived many transitions; it explains the story you told us, Nathaniel. It would seem that he and Stan are more connected than we thought,' Lysis said, addressing Nathaniel who nodded in agreement.

'Yes. It makes perfect sense now. But if that's the case then we have a bigger problem on our hands than just Thrombus and her ever-growing hordes. If the tulpa starts life anew on Earth, then it could mean total annihilation of all souls on Earth, which in turn would wipe us out here,' Nathaniel said gravely. Then he added, 'It really is all my fault. How can I have been so stupid?'

'Will someone please explain to me what a tulpa is, please?' Stan said, feeling impatient.

'Remember when I told you, Stan, essence before existence. Well a tulpa is created from your mind, parallel to your own consciousness. A sentient person who has their own free will that grows with you, feeding off you experiences and learning from them, taking on a persona all of their own. Their emotions and beliefs become their own until they require nothing else from you.'

Stan looked to Lysis, growing more concerned. 'So that's how guardian angels come about then?'

'Well yes, but none have ever been created from one's loss, like it would seem Will has. That explains why he survived and has grown exponentially in power like you.'

'So what affects one of us affects the other too?' Stan said.

'He is the yin to your yang. You interrelate to one another, you are both symbiotic...'

'... and so in doing just that, you have created darkness to your light, one with so much malice and hate, that I shudder to think of what he might accomplish on Earth if he succeeds in reaching there,' Lysis finished.

'So something much more evil than Thrombus and ten times worse could potentially end up on Earth and we're just standing here doing NOTHING!' Stan shouted.

'On the 11th hour comes the end of days! I never

thought it possible,' Ictus said morbidly.

'Stan, you must take Lysis and go to your wife's aid. I feel that my brothers and sister are in mortal danger, now that I have this new information.'

'I'm ready to leave,' Stan said.

Ictus continued, 'Nathaniel will accompany you. If you succeed and I pray that you do, then Lysis, you will become a guardian for Petra, now her guardian has perished and your home is gone.'

Lysis held on to Stan's shoulder in unison. 'I would have it no other way,' he said.

'Nathaniel, you will become gatekeeper to your daughter's oasis, just like Lysis was at Stan's,' Ictus said as he threw his spike to him. 'Stan, I pray you make it home and everything turns out well for you and your fam—'

'But there's more, my oasis is—' Stan interjected.

'No time now. Be off! I can cope here as guardian to your son,' Ictus said, checking under its wings. 'When you return victorious, Nathaniel, then we must talk further about how you actually left paradise. Which is something no soul has ever achieved. I am very keen to know how, so that it does not happen again. For if one can escape so easily, then one can also enter the same.' Ictus said finally.

Nathaniel nodded solemnly. 'Of course.' He took the spike, bowed and then departed with Stan and Lysis, to whatever fate awaited them.

21

FADING LIGHTS

The sleek and nimble leopard lunged for the overbearing canine, shooting out its claws and turning its head to bite down into the dog's mane.

But the dog bent its head in time and with its muscular force, threw itself beneath the leopard and pushed up with all its might, sending the leopard sailing over its back.

Heparin twisted mid-flight and righted himself just as the brute turned back towards him.

Both animals locked eyes and began to circle one another, looking for a weakness in their sparring partner, as they stirred up loose feathers that caught in the wind, to create a whitening blanket around them.

Petra, still wincing in pain, looked on in terror, feeling like she had been invited to a slumber party where a pillow fight had broken out. But this one had turned to violence, leaving her reeling from the scattered, bloody body parts and broken wings of the fallen angels.

The hulking mastiff went to pounce, but stopped mid-way, fooling Heparin into lunging again.

Then the conniving form of Will, extended his

claws and swiped for the face of Heparin, making contact, slicing the sharp talons across the big cat's cheek.

Heparin let out a high-pitched wail, as the nails dug in and found their mark, the force of the swipe spinning his head away.

Then Will was upon him instantly as he sank his fangs into the exposed ruff of Heparin's neck.

*

Having reached the top of the steps, Stan looked to the burning pyre that blew ash around in a swirl, as the wind fed the flames from below, sending the wisps dancing into the night sky.

Nathaniel placed a hand on Stan's shoulder. 'You get a good vantage point from here, look over there to the horizon,' he said, pointing. 'See those two islands? They belong to your daughters... my granddaughters.'

Stan followed Nathaniel's finger and made out the distant shapes. 'I miss them so much,' Stan said, shielding his face from the heat of the fire.

Lysis scuttled up behind them. 'I've just checked on the chasm where the bridge is supposed to be. It's not there anymore! Just the rope railings now. All the boards are missing.'

Nathaniel faced him. 'Did you by any chance, see a net containing a flock of birds near the bridge?'

The large coffin fly looked at him, puzzled. 'No. Should I?'

'It doesn't matter now. Although it is strange. They were still there when I passed earlier with the dark angel... Never mind!' Nathaniel said, disappearing into the treeline.

Peering over the precipice, Stan focused his gaze and saw the frozen waves looming back at him. Then he looked down to the rocky shoreline where the boat lay severed in two.

The heat of the fire felt comforting, but inside Stan felt cold as he rested his sight finally, on the lonely dark figure protecting his son's island.

Stan turned from the bonfire. 'Does this dark angel have a hidden purpose?'

Lysis met Stan's icy stare. 'Ictus, is what some call it on Earth when referring to a sudden stroke of possible death. It does not have a name or gender. It is just a phantom, a harbinger.'

'Can we trust it?' Stan said coldly.

Lysis swivelled his good eye at Stan. 'With your life, if you had one to give. But it has touched you now, as it has sensed your fate. You and Will are too powerful to leave to your own devices.'

Nathaniel reappeared again, scratching his throat. 'This way to the oasis, follow me,' he said hoarsely.

It didn't take long for the trio to find the splintered remains of the picket gate.

They stepped through into what was once the hidden triangular set glade, surrounded by the towering conifers and daisy littered meadow.

The sight that greeted them was of total carnage.

Stan clocked a leopard, pinned down by a large dog who had sunk its fangs into it and was tossing it around like a rag doll.

In that instance Stan knew the leopard was Heparin, his ever-faithful companion.

Readying his sword, Stan was about to aid the

feline, when a female voice cried out, 'Stan! Oh my god! Stan, is that really you? Help me?' she said feebly.

Emotions of relief and regret swept over Stan all at once, as he caught sight of his vulnerable wife. He was momentarily frozen with shock.

The canine, upon hearing the distress call, tossed the leopard into the nearby conifers and manifested into the spectral form of William Last once more.

'Stan, how nice of you to come for the reunion,' Will hissed as he extended his black translucent wings.

Stan, still mesmerised by seeing his wife, didn't have time to act, as Will beat his wings and took off at full speed towards him.

Lysis, who had been anticipating an attack, threw himself into the path of Stan, where he unleashed his tail in a stabbing motion over his back.

The three barbed hooks on Lysis' tail struck home, as Will was impaled in the chest. His screams echoed through the starless night sky.

Lysis turned to Stan. 'See? I told you. As long as you have me, Stan, then there will always be hope,' he said triumphantly.

Then without warning, Will shifted again into his twister-like form, releasing Lysis' barbs.

Lysis, having sensed victory, was suddenly dumbstruck as the swirling vortex picked him up and whisked him away.

The mini tornado went spiralling through the trees and out of sight, taking a spinning Lysis with it, leaving in its wake a large conifer, that came crashing down onto Nathaniel.

Petra's father, having only regained little strength,

THE OASIS OF FEAR

saw the tree topple his way and thrust out his arms to meet it. With a cry of anguish, he broke its fall. Then with a swift motion he slung the tree sideways, where it crashed down onto the corpse of a fallen angel.

He then collapsed to the floor with any remaining energy robbed of him.

Stan, having fought through his momentarily relapse, shouted to Nathaniel to protect Petra at all costs.

Nathaniel waved him away and meekly half smiled, as he looked back remorsefully to his fallen brothers and sister.

Blocking out Petra's obscene protests, Stan turned and fled back through the way of the damaged gate, leaving a sobbing, winded Petra, a wounded Heparin and a fallen Nathaniel, defeated in his mist.

Stan inched further through the trees and strained his ears to any sounds, fearful of an attack, sure that he was being led into a trap. He cursed himself for his lack of judgement and vowed that he would not let anyone or anything hurt his family and friends.

Carefully stepping over broken branches and through rustling bushes, Stan held his sword high, ready to strike at short notice.

He weaved his way through the dense vegetation, occasionally cutting away at any rogue branches that hampered his path, until at last he exited back out onto the cliff's peak.

Stan dropped to his knees, heartbroken.

His sword weighed heavy in his hands, as he let his arm slump to the hard granite floor with a loud clang.

There ahead of him stood the dark and twisted Will.

The evil tulpa of Stan's creation, was warming up his hands, gloating at the cremated remains of Lysis who was alight at the heart of the pyre, the giant coffin fly's light fading away with his very essence.

Feeling rage and hatred build from within, Stan let out a bloodcurdling cry that was carried off by the wind to the dark angel, far off in the distance.

Will turned from the unceremonious act that he had created and strode over to Stan.

'Do not fear, Stan, for once you get back home, this will be a forgotten memory. It will be a time of rejoicing, when I am born into the world with you raising me as your son, along with no knowledge of this ever taking place,' he said, with a delicious, wicked smile.

'YOU WILL NEVER BE MY SON!' Stan raged, as he spat the words at Will.

'But I assure you, I have already won! When I am born again, the world that you know, will bow down to me and there is nothing you can do about it, as you will be oblivious... Dad.'

Stan's hatred had hit boiling point, as he sprang to his feet and thrust the sword at Will, who deftly sidestepped its advance.

'It's time for you to leave, Stan. Quietly or otherwise... it matters not! I will be sure to send my regards to your widow if you choose the latter,' Will said, flashing an evil grin.

Stan struck out. But Will had already blurred into his maelstrom form once more.

'Maybe I will take your daughters from you too,' Will teased.

Stan stepped into the vortex and spun around

anticlockwise to the swirling wind with his sword out. 'OVER... MY... DEAD... BODY!' he screamed.

The angel of death watched on helplessly, as he saw Stan step valiantly into the void and was sucked up into the core of the funnel that was William Last.

As Stan was spun around, jaws of fangs materialised, born of the wind, that began to snap at Stan from every angle and all at once.

Stan slashed wildly at them, but his sword passed through them with every swing.

The chomping mouths snapped at his armoured hide and scraped across its surface as they wrestled to get a grip.

The whirlwind began to shift and carried the spinning, flailing Stan over the side of the cliff, where he hung dangerously over the jagged rocks far below, that housed the two pieces of the little row boat.

Will changed into his winged spectral form, and released Stan, sending him plummeting to his doom. 'See you on the right side!' he shouted after him, as he beat his wings for lift.

Ictus, watching the spectacle unfold as the spinning vortex edged toward the cliff's edge, acted swiftly and pushed his hands into the sea, in anticipation.

The tidal waves that had been frozen by Stan, were released from their hold on touch and melted away, continuing their onslaught once more.

The waves crashed into Petra's island just as Stan was released from Will's grasp.

Stan plummeted into the depths of the tidal wave and was dragged under to the rising split of the row boat below.

Another fading light, extinguished, as he left the prison of his mind once more.

22

WAVE OF DREAD

Stan observed the tenebrosity enclosing around him as the icy cold rush of water consumed him whole.

Struggling to hold on to the fragile threads of his burgeoning mind, Stan submitted to his fate and relinquished his grip, washing away all hope and faith that he could prevent the unstoppable force of Will.

All he had to hold onto now was the evocations of his part here in the oasis, but even they too seemed to be slipping from memory as he swirled in a haze of darkness.

The icy, pitch blackness seemed to inhale and exhale, as if mirroring Stan's own rhythms. It contorted and twisted for Stan, for what felt like an eternity.

When he finally came to, his sight blurred back into focus as the cold, harsh realities of life kicked in once more.

It was as if he was waking from a nightmare.

Stan cupped a hand to his right eye, which streaked away blood from a deep cut that lacerated his brow.

He tried to piece together the remnants of what had befallen him, but an icy blast rattled his senses.

That was when he noticed the gravitas of the situation he now found himself in.

Looking around, Stan could see that he was still in the lifeboat and the tarpaulin that was usually stretched across its surface was now tattered and torn, as it flapped noisily against the battering storm.

Trying to sit up and get a better view, Stan found himself rocking violently in the pendulum motion of the boat, as it slammed against the railings of the ship. One of the large steel arms that held the lifeboat in place had fractured at its join and had been wrenched downwards, creating an uneven hammock for the boat.

Stan pushed his hands and feet out and tried to brace himself within the hull, to stop himself being cast out to the raging torrent below.

Wave after wave buffeted the ship and each time, Stan tried desperately to stop himself sliding out from the hollow of the boat.

He tried to reach out to the thick-set chain that anchored the lifeboat at its bow above his head, but the lashing rain prevented him getting a good grip, as his hand slipped away bitter cold and wet.

That was when he noticed that he had knotted his tie around his wrist.

He must have done it whilst he was unconscious, but he couldn't fathom why. A thought came over him. *Essence before existence.*

What it could possibly mean eluded him, but then a fresh thought ripened in his mind. *Petra is in danger, you must get to her urgently.*

THE OASIS OF FEAR

The slamming of the lifeboat against the rocking of the ship was making Stan feel sick, as he wrestled against each blow. He knew that he had to escape the danger he found himself in, or he would perish in the squall and be swept away to his death, never to be found again.

Stan began to shout for help as he gazed frantically around for a means of escape.

That was when he settled back on the tie around his wrist. If he could loop the loose end through the chain and pull down onto it then it might give him leverage to pull himself out and maybe, just maybe, he could climb across the still intact good steel arm and back to the safety of the ship's deck.

Twisting his face to the rigid chain, Stan scrunched the loose end of his tie in his fist and then cast it free.

The wind whipped it away from its mark and Stan readied himself to throw it again, cursing the storm all around him.

Salty rain hampered his vision as it rinsed the wound above his eye and channelled the blood across his field of view. Stan wiped it with the tie and cast it out once more, but again it missed its mark as he shivered, cold, wet and miserable.

Dread was taking hold. If he did not get out soon, then the lifeboat would be yanked free to the sea along with him on board.

Contorting his body round, Stan again threw the end out; this time he was lucky as the loose end whipped through a chain link, just as the wind changed direction.

With strength of newfound confidence, Stan grabbed a hold and yanked himself up using a thrust from his feet against the hull. It was just in time too, as the left arm finally broke free and sent the aft of the lifeboat swinging loose across the ship's hull.

Stan almost lost his grip as the lifeboat swung into him, knocking away his breath as he strained to hoist himself up.

Lifeboat and man danced backwards and forwards as they spun around one another.

Stan could see the strain on the right steel arm as it too began to fracture, peeling away the white paint from its surface.

A voice echoed from overhead, 'MAN OVERBOARD!'

Stan didn't know whether to laugh or cry as the cliché stung his ears.

Two heads appeared over the railings, belonging to two deck hands who must have been tasked with securing the lifeboat.

The shock of seeing Stan there dangling by his tie, sent the men ashen-faced at the spectacle before them.

A line was cast with a life ring attached to one end; Stan reached out with his left arm and caught it wildly.

He wormed his way through its centre and clung on for dear life as the strain was taken and the deck hands began to pull him up over the sides.

Having finally been dragged back on board the liner, Stan collapsed at their feet and thanked them profusely as they all slipped to and fro on the slippery, wet deck.

'I need to see my wife,' Stan blurted out.

One of the deck hands, a thirty-something young man with ginger hair, said, 'We need to get you to medical first.'

The other bearded deck hand who looked to Stan to be in his forties, wrapped a blanket around Stan and said, 'I agree, first medical and then we can find your wife, sir. I'm afraid we will need to investigate this matter further and we will need a statement from you.'

Stan raised a hand in protest, but no words came out, as the two crew men picked him up and ushered him back to safety inside the ship, towards the medical bay.

23

THE OASIS OF FEAR

Nathaniel hauled himself over to Petra and hugged her tightly. 'Whatever happens here, remember that I will always love you,' he said.

Tears rolled down Petra's face and onto her dad's shoulder. 'I love you too, Daddy,' she wept as she nuzzled in close.

Nathaniel pulled away from the embrace and wiped her tears away. 'I always liked Stan. You bagged yourself a good man there, he will do right by you,' he said.

'I understand why I am here, Dad. But I can't see why Stan is?' Petra said, looking lovingly to her father.

'I know he has been here before, daughter, I can only assume he has had a relapse or worse...' Nathaniel said, through hushed tones.

'Yes, he has. But the doctor treated him with nimodipine. Something else must have happened whilst I've been under,' Petra said, feeling anxious.

'Well whatever it is, I hope you both return safely,' Nathaniel said reassuringly.

A whine and a whimper echoed through the oasis, startling both father and daughter who had both been lost in each other's thoughts.

'The leopard. I'd almost forgot about that,' Nathaniel said, looking over to the big cat as it heaved in shallow breaths under the shadows of the conifer trees.

'Be careful,' Petra said, alarmed.

'Don't you worry about the leopard. It would seem that it was trying to protect you.' Nathaniel said, approaching the cat warily. 'Listen Petra, I need you to gather all those seagulls that are scattered around here for me, okay?' he said, pointing to the lifeless birds that were embedded in his fallen companion and beyond. 'I need their blood to cure our friend here. I need some for myself too if I'm to regain my strength to protect you, in case Stan... well, you know?' Nathaniel trailed off, as he saw his daughter freeze.

Petra was about to say something but thought better of it.

She was used to seeing blood through the many operations she had carried out, but still she felt queasy, as she began to remove the gulls from the hapless victim.

'Why is the leopard here?' Petra said, trying to think of something other than the task she was doing.

'If this big cat is nothing to do with you then I'm guessing it belongs to Stan,' Nathaniel stated, as he hooked the leopard's head over his arm and patted it with his free hand.

Petra approached the pair and dropped the gulls before them, feeling quite nauseous.

Nathaniel bit into one of the birds to release the blood and trickled the crimson fluid into the leopard's wound, healing it over.

'Only thing I can tell then, is that this big cat is symbolic in some way to whatever drug was administered into Stan. What was it called again daughter?'

'Nimodipine. It aids the subarachnoid condition.'

'If that is the case, then Stan may have hope after all! I shall name him Nimodi for short,' he said, grinning.

'You're giving him a name?' Petra said, curling her hair around her finger.

'Every magnificent animal should have a fitting name,' Nathaniel said, smiling at his daughter.

'You sound just like Stan and his naming of our cat, Heparin,' Petra said, bemused.

Nathaniel bit into another gull and began to dine on it. 'This cat of yours, has he by any chance died?' Nathaniel said in between mouthfuls.

Petra, looking on, disgusted, went to answer, when a loud cracking and splintering signalled from afar, striking fear into all three of them.

The leopard Nimodi, raised its head and growled. Finding its voice once more, it rose shakily to its feet and snarled.

Nathaniel ushered Petra behind him and flexed out his almost healed wings, as Nimodi approached his side with his ears pricked back.

The calamity of splintering trees erupted all around them, as the mighty tornado churned up the ground to meet them once again. Then it subsided, as the spectral form of Will materialised. 'That went better than I could have hoped,' he said.

He looked at them all with a menacing glare.

Nathaniel went to make his move, when Petra pulled one of his wings aside and stepped out in front of him.

'No more bloodshed,' she said, trembling.

Nathaniel went to raise a hand in protest, when Petra spoke again. 'No, Dad, I need you here with Nimodi. I give myself over to you, William Last. Just don't hurt them?' she said, looking to her dad regrettably. 'If Stan hasn't made it home, then look out for him, Dad... please?'

'No, Petra, you can't do this,' Nathaniel said with sorrow.

'It is the only way, Daddy. Promise me?' she pleaded.

Nathaniel hugged his daughter and reluctantly stepped aside, pulling the leopard close to him. 'I promise...' he said, restraining the big cat.

Will sneered at Nathaniel and twirled the garland of daisies around his outstretched bony fingers, as he approached the frightened Petra.

He pushed her into the circle of daisies towards the mound and threw the garland over her neck, as he too joined her, and pulled the garland down over his head too.

William then spun back into his torrential whirlwind, that in turn lifted Petra up into its core where she then spun within his contained gale force.

The circle of daisies from the ground were uprooted and they too spiralled upwards, where they created a spinning colourful yellow and white wall.

The mound of earth beneath Petra and Will, began to sink away and created a sinkhole, as Nathaniel and Nimodi gazed on hopelessly.

The swirling voice of Will echoed through the oasis. 'See you in a lifetime... NOT!'

'Not if I see you first,' grunted Nathaniel.

'I doubt that very much,' Will cackled as the hole opened up wider. 'You see, I should have told you before, that beneath the mound lies Thrombus, who is my prisoner. So long as I have her, then I will not be forced back here again. I will feast off her malice and nurture her evil to use on Earth. I won't need to return... EVER! I will be immortal.'

Nathaniel watched the vortex sink down into the abyss, taking his daughter away from sight. 'But you WILL have to, William, for Thrombus is no longer your captive. She was slain by the angel of death,' he said defiantly.

'NO! It cannot be,' wailed Will, as the vortex vanished into the ground, bringing the wall of daisies flowing down upon it. It then sealed over again with earth, masking Will's cries and sealing the portal like a cork in a bottle.

'Yes, William. I will see you in a lifetime. I will be waiting for you... I will make you suffer!' Nathaniel said, as he plucked up a nearby daisy and laid it on the mound of earth.

*

The dark angel, having witnessed the downfall of Stan, knew it was only a matter of time, as it waited as acting sentry over the unborn child. Its keen hearing had picked up the passing conversations from afar and knew the terrible deed was done.

All it could do now was amass an army and be ready for the tulpa's return.

A gurgling sound reverberated beneath it.

Ictus stood up and looked down into the birthing canal of the foetus.

The water within drained away and plunged the sac containing the child into its dark abyss.

Sand then tumbled in after it, as it sealed shut, glassing over any remnants that the birthplace had even existed.

A sapling began to shoot through the surface, as its leaves unfurled to the elements.

The dark angel wondered if a black rose would mature, or that of a daisy. It knew only time would tell, as it prayed for the latter.

But first it would need to seek council and then collect the free spirit of the children, for they would be needed to bridge the return of Stan safely.

Nothing could be left to chance now.

The oasis of fear was no more, but the oasis of life was just beginning.

The dark angel hoped that the light would illuminate the darkness from the unborn child and shine through... or else damnation of the populace on Earth would spread like a virus.

One with no cure.

24

A TO B NEGATIVE

'Ladies and gentleman, this is the captain's announcement! We have now passed through the storm and all facilities are now returning to normal. You are now permitted to leave your cabins and muster stations. Your destination is now only two hours away until disembarkment. Thank you.'

Cheers from all passengers on board greeted the air, except from those in the medical bay, where a surprised Stan had found an unconscious Petra being tended by nurses only moments earlier.

Having established that Stan was a suitable donor for Petra and having had his blood tested, Doctor Erikson had proceeded to start the transfusion process.

Doctor Erikson looked over his rimmed glasses to Stan as he tied off the tourniquet around his arm. 'Preparations are now under way, Mr Palmer, and as soon as we have Mrs Palmer stabilised then we can transport you both to the helipad to fly you on to the nearest land-based hospital, where you will both be better treated.'

Stan went to respond but winced, as Nurse Tanya dabbed away at the cut above his eye with a saline solution.

Doctor Erikson inserted the needle into Stan's arm and checked that the cannula was hooked up to the drip.

Satisfied that all was working well, Doctor Erikson put a reassuring hand to Stan's shoulder. 'All will be fine, Mr Palmer, your wife is strong willed and I'm sure everything will be okay once the medics on the mainland have her. I was worried that the very rare AB negative blood that you and your wife share, would not be matched by any other passengers aboard the whole of this ship.' Then he added, 'But luckily you are both a match. I thought the odds would be greatly stacked against us, seems I was wrong.'

Stan pressed upon the plaster that Tanya had applied above his eye. 'Thank you, Doc, and thank you, Nurse. Yes, we were both surprised to learn that we shared the same blood group, but until now I hadn't given it much thought,' he said, feeling numb and cold.

Tanya put a cold compress to Petra's forehead and wiped away at her long strands of hair. 'How on earth did you end up out there on the lifeboat anyway?' she said, looking concerned at Stan.

Shrugging it off in a nonplussed manner, Stan gazed longingly at the still unconscious Petra. 'Will the baby be okay?' he said tenderly.

Tanya frowned at Stan but carried on with her chores regardless.

Doctor Erikson raised an eyebrow at Stan. 'They will both be fine. It is you I am more concerned about now. You must take the medicine that I have prescribed, Mr Palmer, and more importantly, I must stress that you do not drink alcohol as a substitute! Do you understand the ramifications if you do?' he said in a scolding tone.

'Yes Doc, I do and I will keep up the meds... I promise,' Stan said, trying to hide his shaking hands. 'I love my wife unconditionally and will try my best to be strong for all of us,' he added sympathetically to the doctor's approval.

As the transfusion was concluded and preparation for their removal got under way, Stan found himself lost once again in thought as they were trundled off to the waiting helicopter.

His head was still hazy as he tried to piece together hidden memories that taunted him from the dark recess of his mind.

None of this was coincidental, of that he was sure, but it eluded him as to the inner meanings of it all. For some reason, although he was happy that Petra was now out of harm's way, he did not feel the same way towards his unborn son.

Warning signs signalled in his mind's eye, alerting him of clear and present danger.

There was just no way he could feel empathy or love for the child; he hated himself for thinking this way.

His thoughts turned once again to having a stiff drink when all this was over, a small blessing in the grand scheme of life.

Maybe soothing his thoughts was the best cure to deal with the stress, that bringing a new child into the world could mean.

He would unravel his secreted away thoughts one way or another someday, for that hopefully would hold the key to putting this unfortunate turn of events behind him.

Putting his thoughts behind him for now, Stan watched Petra be lifted into the chopper and climbed in behind her, leaving what he hoped were his troubles and woes truly behind him, as their otherwise romantic but life-affirming holiday came to an end.

25

MEDICINAL PURPOSES

Three weeks later...

Stan arrived at the hospital by car, clutching a gerbera daisy celebration bouquet, adorned with pink roses, pink gerbera daisies, pink alstroemeria and purple monte casino.

Dustin exited the car first and opened the door for Stan, merely as a force of habit for the chauffeuring service he had been accustomed to in his time of working for the funeral service.

Natasha killed the engine and removed the keys before locking the car by the fob and hastily tagging along behind them, holding Petra's overnight bag.

'Big day then, Stan, bet you're excited for the first day of holding Nathan Palmer properly, aren't you?' Natasha said, catching up to them.

Stan eyed her cautiously. 'We haven't quite settled on a name yet, Natasha,' he said, hurrying towards the emergency doors, trying to hide his solemn mood.

'I like the name Wesley myself,' Dustin said as he swung the doors open for his two companions.

'Oh, babe, that's a bit old fashioned,' Natasha said, as she passed by courteously.

'That's my late dad's name!' Dustin said, hurt, as he let the doors swing shut behind them, rushing to catch up.

'I know that name from somewhere else, don't I?' Stan said as he approached the reception desk.

Dustin went to answer when Natasha interjected. 'Sorry hun, I didn't know, we haven't had a chance to...' she trailed off in hushed words.

'That's fine, another time,' Dustin replied, as he slipped an arm around her waist.

'Come on. This way, you two,' Stan said, having acquired the information from the nurse at the desk. 'They're both awake and Petra has already fed the boy apparently, so you're both welcome in,' he said, sharing the update as he led the way.

'Where are the girls?' Natasha asked.

'They left an hour ago, I received a text earlier. Sorry, should have told you,' Stan said apologetically.

'That's fine, sweetie, no big deal. I will see them soon, I'm sure,' Natasha said, as Stan opened the door to Petra's ward.

Stan's mood lifted when he clapped eyes on his wife sitting up in bed, but as his eyes caught sight of his sickly-looking son, his mood wavered again.

He approached Petra and gave her an awkward hug and a kiss on the cheek. 'We got some bits together for you, darling,' he said, pulling away to retrieve the bag from Natasha.

Having placed it on the side cabinet, Stan accidentally knocked over some well-placed well-wisher's cards. He cursed himself for trying to hide his shakes and the ill feeling he felt.

As he stooped over to scoop them up, he was eagerly pushed aside, as Natasha began to coo and ahh at the baby.

Stan gathered the cards and mindlessly opened them up one by one, taking very little notice of what each card had to say, before he reassembled them around the room.

Dustin approached him and slung a thumbs-up over his shoulder to the women and baby behind him. 'When we're done here, do you want to go wet the baby's head down the local, Stan?'

Stan brought his finger up to his lips. 'Sshh, I don't want Petra getting worried that I'm going to have a drink. As far as she knows, I haven't touched a drop in weeks,' Stan said, whispering.

'Oh, okay. Sorry Stan, I just thought that she wouldn't mind under these circumstances,' Dustin said, abashed.

Petra, overhearing titbits of their conversation, spoke up. 'No way, Dustin, is Stan allowed to go with you to the pub. I expect you to take him straight home when visiting time's up,' she said, giving Stan a firm nod.

'That's fine, darling, I will be walking home after hours here,' Stan said, feeling for the hard hip flask tucked away in his winter coat.

'But it's cold out with frost on the ground. You will catch your death of cold,' Natasha said, nuzzling the baby close.

'I'm fine, honest,' Stan said, forcing a smile.

'So long as you're sure, Stan,' Dustin said, pretending he didn't see Stan fondling his pocket.

'Yup, all good,' Stan said as he made his way over

to the bed.

Natasha passed the baby over to Stan as he got himself comfortable and returned to having a deep conversation with Petra.

Dustin sat down next to Stan. 'He has your eyes,' he said, holding out his finger for the baby to grip hold of.

Stan looked at his son, but all affection was lost on him as they regarded one another.

Stan sensed that his son was in there somewhere but just not today. It was like it was someone else's child, but he couldn't fathom out why he thought that.

He guessed that he should keep those dark thoughts to himself.

Petra looked upon them lovingly in between her conversations with Natasha, but she sensed too that Stan was not himself. In fact, since returning from their trip, Stan had almost become a recluse again and was keeping himself to himself.

She figured that he was blaming himself for what had happened on board, but no matter how hard she tried, she could not get him to open up his feelings.

She was afraid that he wasn't being over truthful with her on taking his medication or his supposed drinking habits that were now under control, in his words.

But Petra knew she had to put herself and the baby before Stan.

She figured that maybe Stan was feeling pushed out by her son's arrival, but she couldn't be sure.

She would make things alright once they were all reunited back home, as one big happy family. It was just the separation by circumstance that was making life difficult at the moment, she assured herself.

Finally visiting hours were up and Natasha and Dustin said their farewells.

Dustin made sure Stan was still okay with walking home and said to be careful on the way, as the cold winter sun wasn't melting the ice away quick enough.

Stan mumbled something that Dustin couldn't make out.

Dustin went to leave, then halted at the door. 'By the way, Stan, I almost forgot. I've got a little something for you to give to the babe when he's older!' he said, slipping out a gift-wrapped tube, from within his inner breast pocket. Dustin handed Stan the sealed gift. 'It was something that was handed down to me by my father on his passing. I thought you'd appreciate it.'

Natasha took Dustin's hand in hers. 'Oh, hun, that's a lovely gesture,' she said, planting a kiss on his cheek.

Stan received the gift. 'Thanks, I'll open it later if that's okay?'

'Sure thing, I'd prefer that,' Dustin said, before leading Natasha out the door. Then they were off.

Stowing the gift in his oversized pockets, Stan waved them goodbye and turned back to the room, and picked up his child from Petra's arms.

Stan placed the unfamiliar child within the cot and gave Petra a big hug and a kiss. 'I miss you,' he said.

'I miss you too and I worry about you,' Petra said, hugging him tightly.

'I'm fine. Besides, the girls are keeping me

company at home, so you needn't worry, love,' Stan said, feeling somewhat warm under her embrace.

'It's my job to worry, promise me you will be good?' Petra said.

'I will... I love you. Make sure you get some rest, you look exhausted,' Stan said wholeheartedly.

'I love you too and yes I will,' Petra said.

Stan got up and went to leave when Petra added, 'What about Nathan? Are you not going to say goodbye to your son too?'

'Yeah, sure I am,' Stan said, approaching the cot reluctantly.

He leaned in and kissed the sleeping baby's head. 'Love you, little one. Be safe,' he said, feeling the guilt wash over him.

Before Stan exited the room, he turned back to Petra. 'I like the name Nathan, a strong name like your father's, only shorter.'

Tears rolled down Petra's cheeks. 'Good, then I am glad that's settled. Nathan Palmer, it is.'

Stan blew Petra a kiss goodbye, then left the hospital into the soft, warm glow of the low hanging winter sun.

He pulled out his untouched nimodipine bottle of pills and tossed them into the nearest bin, not even hesitating for a second.

Then he slipped out his hip flask, unscrewed the lid and swigged down the soothing warmth of the whiskey until the flask was totally empty.

He looked at the engraving on the flask it read:

TO STAN
THE GREATEST SON IN LAW
IN THE WORLD. I COULDN'T
WISH FOR A BETTER MAN
TO LOOK AFTER MY
PRECIOUS DAISY

Stan had a flashback of Nathaniel dressed in white garbs with wings sprouting from his back. It was as if the flask was a gentle reminder of something else, something that Stan had witnessed whilst he was passed out in the lifeboat.

The pieces were beginning to make sense, but it scared Stan half to death as to what he might unravel. The flask shook against his unsteady grip.

This medicine had indeed served a purpose, one that Stan was afraid to reveal the truth of, but one that he knew he must.

He knew somehow the rest of the answers would be found at the beginning of all his troubles.

He stashed the flask back in his pocket and made the long slippery walk towards the Mala Sort River, for reasons that even he could not comprehend.

26

VESSEL INCARNATE

Petra's island of her mind was flooded with angels of all races, from all walks of previous lives, men and women combined, congregating far and wide across the cliffs and rolling fields as far as the eye could see, with a crowd spilling over across the sand bank to the blossoming of Nathan Palmer's island.

Ictus had summoned as many as it could without leaving the numbers too short in the waging war far off in the distance.

A council was being held in Petra's private sanctuary of her hidden oasis, that had been fortified immensely since her departure.

At the centre of the council sat Nathaniel with Nimodi flaked out beside him in the midday sun, along with the dark angel itself, who was addressing a large circle of angels that had formed around them.

'Nothing happens in life by chance. There has and will always be a higher purpose than mere mortals can comprehend. Every action has a consequence and every consequence has a deeper meaning for the shaping of the journey that lies ahead,' the dark angel began.

Whispers spread amongst the listeners.

'Call it fate or destiny, call it what you like, but the outcome will follow them here eventually. There is a child that has been born into the world, one whose soul has been spliced with another. An evil tulpa that has found a way to break free from the afterlife and spread back into the fresh soil of the earth to taint it with malice.'

The whispers broke into loud chattering.

'My kin, be silent,' Ictus said, with grand presence.

The chatter subsided once more as the angels stared at one another in disbelief.

'This tulpa is more evil than the queen Thrombus herself, who will always be a growing concern here with her invading armies. But that pales in comparison with the evil that has now washed up on Earth. At the moment, the child is in a happy balance, but that could change as it becomes mature. I along with Nathaniel have stopped it being born evil by eradicating Thrombus before it made its transition to Earth, but I fear that if transgression or an outside influence was to interfere with the child's life, then we could experience end of days as we know it. Everything here could be in vain if we do not succeed back in the birthplace of Earth.'

The angels broke into a loud argument of shock and horror as the true meaning hit home.

One of the angels spoke out. 'How do we prevent this from happening then? What can we do to ensure that the child has a fair chance? Surely it is against our beliefs to interfere with the moral choices a soul makes?'

Nathaniel cleared his raspy throat and spoke. 'My

grandson has been robbed of a normal life, before he even starts his journey. I promise you we have put plans into motion to prevent events going against us, but we must work together,' he said, stroking the mane of fur along Nimodi's back.

'But how can you be sure that it is spliced with a tulpa? It is not unheard of for souls to be reborn. It is not a common occurrence but it does happen, and although whilst the soul is young, there is confliction with its new parents. In time that becomes a fading memory, surely?' the angel replied.

Ictus spoke once more. 'We cannot and will not take that chance. The only problem is time. We will have to wait for the child to come of age before we act, but only one can make that decision, only one can alter the cause of the soul's path and that is the boy's father. He is the one who wields a power so great that I have never witnessed it before.'

The crowd of angels erupted into questions and doubts once more, as their wings beat fervently against their backs.

The leopard yawned and rolled over as it batted away an irksome fly that kept landing on its face.

Nathaniel gave Nimodi's belly a good rub and stood up. 'A long time ago a friend of mine called Lysis, once told me that no one is an island, we all need to be around someone. Loneliness is the killer. With support and understanding I believe we can all do our part.' He opened his arms and looked around at all his fellow angels. 'We know the town and location of my grandson's birthplace and that is where you will all keep watch and manipulate the outcome unseen, until Nathan Palmer comes of age. You will report back and exchange information of his whereabouts at all times.'

'Why should we believe what a fallen has to say? Wasn't it you that tried to be reborn yourself? Wasn't it you that started this all off?' another angel said bitterly.

'I was wrong. I see that now and yes, I feel ashamed for my actions, but I swear an oath today that I will make this right, with or without your help,' Nathaniel said imploringly. 'My son-in-law will bring the joined souls here unscathed and we will split them apart and send my grandson back unhurt, and deal with this tulpa in person. Now, the vessel is pure, but in time it may become a vessel incarnate if we fail. I can only hope that my grandson grows to believe that this tulpa is just an imaginary friend and in time will come to abandon it, as all children do with their toys eventually,' Nathaniel said, cupping his hands in prayer.

'What of the boy's father? Where is he?' a different angel said from beyond the throng.

Nathaniel sounded upset and deflated when he spoke once again. 'Still on Earth... but not for long. He is nearing his Earth journey's end. He just doesn't know it yet! It is too dangerous to leave him unchecked on the earth whilst this plays out, so we have sent for him. He is now piecing it all together and when he does and the last piece falls into place, then the bell will chime for him.'

The dark angel, sensing Nathaniel's grief, reached out and gripped his arm, as it looked to the party of angels before it. 'Other than those instructed to stay, the rest of you will approach an oasis of your choice from the millions on offer and you will make your way to Earth. You will be our eyes and ears. Also, be aware of evil acting against us there. God speed,' it said, before outstretching its mighty razored wings and turning away.

'I wish to speak with Stanley Palmer when he arrives, for there is much to discuss. He will have many questions too. I besiege you to direct those questions to me and me alone, do not answer them yourself, Nathaniel,' Ictus said.

'As you wish,' Nathaniel responded, clapping his thigh for Nimodi to join him.

'One last thing, Nathaniel. Please do not speak of your escapade of leaving paradise through the eclipse to anyone. It is our secret only, do you understand?'

Nathaniel looked to the menacing sight of the angel of death darkly and gulped. 'Yes, I understand,' he said, as he massaged his throat.

With a great flapping of wings and loose feathers sent swirling into the wind, the flock of disillusioned and fearful angels took to the skies, blotting out the sun.

Onwards to destination Earth, the angels flew, leaving Nathaniel worried for the welfare of his daughter, his precious little daisy, who was soon to be a widow.

In the distance, Stan's island had almost succumbed to the depths of the ocean bed as it made its descent from view.

27

A REQUIEM FOR STANLEY PALMER

Standing on the misty banks of the Mala Sort River, Stan had his eyes closed to the low winter sun that saturated a hazy orange glow through his eyelids.

The river smoke drifted in swirls across the watery channel, obscuring the ice that formed out and around the bull rush that gathered in wide patches across its span.

Stan pulled his hands from his pockets and cupped them to his face, as he blew warm breath to stop them freezing. He returned a hand to his pocket and pulled out the cold steel flask.

Remorse descended over him as he studied it, lost in thought.

Deciding there and then that he would take back control of his life, he threw the flask through the haze into the slow flow of the river, where it splashed into the icy depths, breaking the eerie silence.

He was done with drink and prescription drugs, for all they ever did was to numb his senses. Now was a time of clarity.

Stan felt an epiphany, as it dawned on him that he

had been his own worst enemy.

The accident that had caused his guilt and his phobia had almost claimed his life since that dreadful day.

Subarachnoia had almost taken him a second time, but it was the demon drink that almost consumed him, that and the stubbornness he had, on not taking his wife's advice by taking his medication.

But no more! The visions were overwhelming and too compelling to ignore. He had to recollect his memories as if driven by an unseen urgency to uncover a dark secret that he possessed.

He walked along the bank and crunched through the frozen dew drops that hung off the unkempt grass, checking his watch. It was 5.45pm. Another 15 minutes and the church would ring its bells.

Up ahead rested the bench that was erected in honour of his fallen classmates who had perished in the river when he was a child.

Stan's mood was melancholy by the time he reached it.

He removed his scarf and wiped the frost off the seat and across the backrest, where he found himself polishing the plaque. When he was satisfied that the brass was shiny and almost feeling like he had rubbed his troubles away, Stan folded up the scarf and placed it onto the seat.

He sat down upon the bench, to glance at the wonderful but surreal alien landscape, that made him feel more alive than he had ever felt.

Passing traffic from behind and far above the slope, interrupted his thoughts briefly, before he turned back to the calm and tranquil beauty before him.

In the distance Stan could make out a small group of children playing down by the river.

He couldn't believe how irresponsible some parents could be for the welfare of their kids. Out on their own, playing down by a dangerous river that had already claimed young unfortunate souls long before now.

Reaching into the deep pocket of his sheepskin coat, Stan felt for the cylindrical gift that Dustin had bestowed upon him earlier.

He picked away at the blue paper with its pattern of colourful balloons emblazoned across it and tore the paper off in strips.

Peering into the cardboard tube that revealed itself, Stan saw something was rolled up within it.

Tipping the tube upside down and giving it a forceful shake, a rolled-up comic was ejected from its hollow, where Stan caught its fall with his free hand.

Unfurling the comic, a sudden surge of shock coursed through Stan's veins.

THE INCREDIBLE ADVENTURES OF THE HUMAN COFFIN FLY #3 edition comic was in his grasp.

Over time the pulp had been dried out and the pages had been carefully prised apart, almost restoring it back to its original state.

There was no doubt in Stan's mind that Dustin had given him back his comic from his youth.

The one that had caused the accident, the one that Stan had thought was lost to time, along with the deceased passengers of the minibus.

But how? Why now? Stan thought, as palpitations

crept across his chest.

Then, like a final part of the puzzle had been completed, Stan realised its significance.

Dustin, was the son of the minibus driver!

He said the gift was passed to him by his father, Wesley.

Stan remembered now that when he and Petra had read the obituaries, whilst Stan overcame his guilt, that they had revealed the driver to be named Wesley. So Dustin must have been handed it upon the funeral of his dad.

But if that's the case, then that must mean that the hearse accident and Dustin meeting Natasha was by no means coincidence, Stan thought, trying to make sense of it.

Then a darker thought came to him. *What if Natasha told Dustin of his guilt in causing the accident. Would Dustin want revenge? Would he want justice for a robbed youth?*

Stan then found his head swimming, as his temples throbbed.

Oh God! Could it be that Dustin poisoned Heparin? he thought, alarmed. *Could my family be in danger?*

Suddenly and as if on cue, all Stan's memories of what had occurred came flooding back to him.

The fight with the Virchow's triad. The showdown with Thrombus, William Last's betrayal. The tulpa, William now reincarnated here on Earth... in guise of his son! Also and equally as important, his friend Lysis, the magnificent coffin fly. His fallen friend... his saviour!

Stan found himself in a daze, as warm tears rolled down his cheeks and landed softly on the image of the incredible coffin fly that was posed heroically on the comic's cover.

Stan's world was turned upside down as he was thrown topsy-turvy into a blind panic.

Wandering around in a blur, Stan went to make for the stiles that led away from the river and back up to the road, when something pulled him back by his coat tail.

The children he had witnessed down by the river moments ago had now gathered around him.

One of them, a boy, was pulling Stan back. There was no denying who it was – it was Adron.

'Don't go, Stan. You belong with usss. It isss time to go. Come home, Stan. Join usss,' he said in a playful way.

Stan's mind raced, seeing the dead-eyed children. 'But I'm not ready, I have to warn Petra,' Stan said, feeling uneasy on his feet.

But the children's hold over him was too strong. They were his fallen classmates and his place was with them now. Just as they were claimed a long time ago, they were now here to claim his soul. Stan's half-life was going to expire.

A sense of nirvana took hold, as Stan's anchor to life was undone.

His eyes glossed over a milky, white sheen, as a stroke took hold, along with the children that freed him from the world.

A requiem for Stanley Palmer's memories played out as his body crumpled and rolled down into the icy Mala Sort River.

The church on the hill rang out the first of its six

chimes in the distance. *Bong...*

Not even the chill of the river would revive him now.

Bong... Bong... The children waded in to join him.

The noise echoed in Stan's final thoughts. *Bong... Bong...*

Stan's soul separated from his body, leaving an empty husk behind.

His soul rose up to join with the children. *Bong!*

The future uncertain, the path ahead unknown.

The physical connection to Earth, well and truly severed.

Read on for an exciting preview of
THE OASIS OF LIFE
The final instalment of the Oasis trilogy
by Matthew Newell

A FIEND IN NEED

The widow Petra Palmer, rested against her dusty and grease-caked worktop, lost deep in thought in her small but modest kitchen.

Pots and pans half filled with stagnant water piled high in the sunken sink beside her. But keeping on top of household chores was the last thing on her mind, as she stood there in her dream-like state.

Her cell phone vibrated noisily into life and begun to violently shake across the dusty surface of the matte black worktop, leaving a jagged path. It sifted through the thick powder in its wake, making its way across to the recess of the stainless-steel sink that was coated in a milky white film.

Not giving the phone a single glance, Petra replayed past events over and over in her mind as if she was trying to make sense still, of what had happened to lead her up to this point in time now.

Eight years ago, can that length of time really have passed so quick in a blink of an eye? she thought, as her eyes welled up to the pain of her late husband Stanley Palmer's passing.

Today was the anniversary of his death, but now only a cold, empty void remained in her heart where warmth and love once overflowed in abundance for him.

To make matters worse, it was hard to disguise her sunken, solemn mood, that echoed that of the pouring rain which battered the kitchen window from outside, when she should still be celebrating her son Nathan's eighth birthday, which was only two days past.

Leaning against the worktop, she twirled within her left hand strands of her matted hair that had now weathered grey and had lost all sheen and radiance, draping unkempt about her shoulders.

In her right hand she mindlessly toyed with a crystal glass pendant that hung from a silver chain around her neck, that had infused in its centre, a striking depiction of a lone daisy. The pendant was cold but soothing to the touch as she tried to focus her mind.

The last time Petra had seen Stan alive was when he had visited her and baby Nathan in hospital, which had been a very joyous occasion.

The journey up until that moment had been tainted with much pain and suffering, but the birth of Nathan had swept all the anguish away and had drawn Petra and Stan closer, appreciating the bond of their increasing family, as they had two daughters already. A son was what Petra knew was needed to fulfil their lives more.

But Petra knew her husband only too well and on that same night, she had sensed Stan was harbouring a very dark secret, that unfortunately he would take to his grave as he left the ward and their lives forever.

Stanley Palmer had reoccurring health issues, with a brain tumour that had put him into a coma a couple of years earlier, from a dreadful accident by the Mala Sort River close to where they lived.

He had endured his fight and awoken from his agonising sleep, but was never the same man he used to be. For although his recovery thereafter was good, Petra knew that the path to wellness was beset with relapses that Stan was trying his best to hide from her.

As a practicing neurosurgeon, Petra knew only too well the battles that lay ahead for the both of them, but any slight pressure and concerned nagging she gave him, would be tough for her husband, she knew, as he was a proud man who liked to take on the world in his own way and not have to let his family suffer for him.

Eventually on that cold and bleak night, he had exited the building and had taken a walk down to the Mala Sort River again. The destination was the last journey he would have taken when his brain had finally shut down.

Petra bit her bottom lip in frustration for her foolishness for not seeing the signs earlier. *If only things had gone better between our breakdown in conversation, then maybe Stan would still be here now.*

Her pregnancy with Nathan though, had zapped her of energy. Along with a hard labour, she almost died as a result of pre-eclampsia whilst they had been on holiday.

She and Nathan had survived that turmoil, so she found it hard to believe that Stan could give up so easily.

How futile life cam truly be, she thought.

The bittersweet taste of the syrupy blood trickled down her throat, leaving a metallic tang behind as she recounted that later that night and some hours later, she had an unexpected visit from the on-duty nurse in tow, with two police officers looking very timid and bearing grave news.

Petra had been happily breastfeeding Nathan when they came hurrying in and had to quickly snatch Nathan's mouth from her breast in haste to cover up her modesty.

The news of her late husband's demise still echoed loudly in her thoughts as the shocking event plagued her soul.

She was told there and then, with trepidation from the officers, that Stan must have had an accident, for there seemed no foul play was at work.

A jogger had been out running alongside the frosty banks of the river when he had spotted Stan's body face-down in the centre of the iced-over stretch of water, frozen in time, on what would be the coldest night on record.

Oh, how she missed him, she never wanted him to go that way. *He must have been so lonely out there all by himself.*

Everything that had come after, from the housekeeping, to balancing work and raising Nathan, had been numb and agonising.

It was at times like these today that she wished her dad Nathaniel was here to hug her. He though, had long since passed away and now only his shortened name belonging to her son remained. At least she and Stan had agreed on their son's name on that occasion, for she knew he could be difficult at times to agree to anything.

At least Petra still had two daughters to support her, even though her youngest, Sally, had a family of her own, and Anastasia was trying for one with her husband, they both had busy work lives to attend to, but were more than willing to lend support. They even made the effort to babysit every so often.

Fishing out her now silent, soggy phone from the sink, Petra dried the screen on her sweater and swiped to unlock it, looking at the name of the missed call. It was from Dustin who was a close friend of the family, who had once upon a time dated Stan's boss Natasha, who also had been a rock to her in those early days of grief.

But Natasha and Dustin's relationship never lasted, for reasons still unknown to Petra to this day.

Like all good things, Petra figured, everything must come to an end one day. Death in its many forms would always break up a party.

She wondered if afterlife truly existed, and that if it did, would it heal her broken heart when she was finally reunited with her soulmate...? She prayed that it would.

Putting the phone to standby, Petra returned it to the worktop and reached for her preferred brand of cigarette that was half smouldering in the ashtray that she had absentmindedly forgotten was there.

She brought the butt up to her lips to take a drag, but the pain of the hot nicotine stung her open wound and forced her to throw it into one of the pots of water with a hiss.

Glancing to the outside rain that lashed the window, Petra brought up her sweater sleeve and wiped the fresh blood away.

Condensation built up on the inside of the glass of the window and slightly obscured the haggard reflection of herself within.

Trickles of water bubbled through the rotten-framed window as another stale thought came into her mind.

The day of Stan's funeral had been chaotic and was steeped in so much negativity that Petra had prayed that the long day would just end, or the cemetery would just swallow her whole.

From the hearse getting a puncture en route, to the sodden coffin being dropped just shy of the catafalque, that dark day was a nightmare of horrors.

Nathan's demands and constant crying had been the only real thing that made sense to her in the calamity that ensued, for inside herself she was screaming at the top of her lungs, *Why, God, is this happening to me?!*

Time, as it always did, moved on, but Petra's scars were still on show for all to see. Dustin over time had grown very close to her and Nathan, as she and Natashia had grown further apart.

Petra guessed that it must have been Dustin's guilt that made him hang around, as he happened to work in the funeral industry as a regular hearse driver, who in possession of Stan's body at his funeral that day, seemed to carry the brunt of all the things that had gone wrong.

The funeral had been delayed by twenty minutes as the hearse had a wheel blow out and Dustin and the conductor had to quickly change it at the side of the road.

Dustin's knuckles were bleeding profusely by the time a fresh tyre was mounted on, as his hands had scraped the surface of the road in removing the dud tyre.

To top it off for Dustin, when he brought Stan's coffin into the crematorium as pallbearer, he twisted his ankle whilst carrying the load and fell to the floor in agony. The coffin slid away from the other three pallbearers and crashed into his ribs, sending out a large resounding echo around the chapel as the heavy coffin then hit the marbled floor, muffling his screams. The looks of the shocked congregation still haunted Petra today.

It was like Stan had it in for him, Dustin had guessed, but never shared his thoughts with Petra, for he did after all, kill Stan's pet cat and was there just before Stan died, when he had confronted him about the death of his own father which he blamed on Stan, when Stan was but a child.

Dustin's dad had been the minibus driver who ferried Stan and a few of his fellow pupils to and from school. But one day, Stan had caused Dustin's dad to veer off road, which resulted in the bus careering down the gorge and out into the rapids of the Mala Sort River, where all but one soul had perished... Stan had been the only survivor.

So there was Dustin now, getting his comeuppance, with his partner Natasha, who was attending and seated nearby in the crematorium and who was still very much his partner at the time, pleading for her to help.

She raced over to join all those already in the struggle involved, clumsily trying their best to get the coffin to its resting place, which was worse for wear, with the flower spray now higgledy-piggledy and askew on the top of the casket. Dustin was amazed that he still had a job after that day.

Stan, whose soul had not long said farewell to the world, had indeed been orchestrating the enfolding events from beyond the grave, but his energy was not quite yet harnessed to do harm to Dustin as he had envisioned.

It was like he was on the wrong side of the door, for death was just the beginning of a soul's journey.

Eight years later and to Stan's great comfort whilst he bided his time in the Astral plane, that existed between Earth and Paradise, something wonderful had happened. Petra had turned Stan's ashes into a daisy pendant that she now wore around her neck that also served her, without knowing, to work as a tether that linked the world he found himself in to our world.

Stan was pleased, as the pendant acted as a talisman that would ward off evil and allow him to reach out in subtle ways to connect to the earth and his wife, including that of the advances from Dustin towards his wife.

As for the rest of Stan's ashes, they were encased in an urn to be buried later with some left over, waiting to be transferred into three fireworks that Stan had requested in his will, be shot up into the sky above the town where he grew up.

It was Dustin's confession of his guilt that tore his relationship with Natasha apart many months later, as he implored her forgiveness and to keep his dark secret, which she did to the present day. But the forgiveness Dustin sought would never, ever come; in the end they went their heartbroken, separate ways.

A key struck the lock to the front door and rattled in the casing, bringing Petra back to reality from her dark past.

'If you go then, Nathan, and make sure you take your raincoat straight off to hang up and whilst you're at it, get out of those wet shoes before you leave the hallway to go see Mummy,' a cheery voice said from behind a large brown umbrella that was being shaken free of water.

Petra tucked the pendant back into her yellow sweater, wiped her tears and stepped out into the hallway.

On seeing Nathan bounding toward her, she bent down and scooped him up into her arms before nuzzling his neck, which caused him to giggle.

'How's my favourite boy?' she asked, looking over his shoulder to the figure stepping through the threshold to hang up the now closed umbrella.

'He was as good as gold, I think he enjoys being with his Uncle Dustin as much as I enjoy looking after him,' the figure replied in answer to her open question.

The pendant beneath Petra's thick sweater slightly shimmered.

Nathan uncoupled from his mum then darted off around her to switch on the television in the adjacent living room.

Dustin removed his damp coat and slung it casually over the stair bannister and approached Petra to give her a big hug and a kiss to the cheek.

An overhanging light bulb popped in its fitting and

showered Dustin in fine glass dust.

'Damn! I keep telling you that you could do with a handyman around here. I'm more than happy to help,' Dustin said, noticing Petra's dried, streaked cheeks.

Petra lightly pushed him away. 'Thank you, Dusty,' she said, turning away from him to go retrieve a cigarette.

'You going to be alright? Or would you like some company tonight?' Dustin said, following her into the kitchen.

A photo of Stan, Petra and their two daughters encased in its frame fell off the wall in the living room, alerting Nathan, who went to pick it up.

Petra, startled by the noise it made when it hit the floor, turned to Dustin. 'I don't think it's a good idea today, Dusty. You know what day it is. I think it's best that I spend some time alone with Nathan today... But thank you for taking him out for a while. I do appreciate it,' she said, lighting up and ignoring the pain from her lip.

Dustin threw open his hands. 'Sure, no problem. You know I'm happy to help you out any time,' he said, looking into her hollow eyes.

Petra went to walk into the living room to take the photo from Nathan when Dustin grabbed her shoulder. 'Are we still on for me moving into the guest room? Because I'm all packed and ready to move in. Then I can pay my way and get this house back to some kind of normality,' he said, looking at the unwashed dishes and rotten window frame that had painted splinters of wood peeling away.

'Soon,' Petra said, then added, 'I just need a little

more time to adjust.'

'Okay, that's fine. Just give me a call when you're ready,' he said, retreating back down the hallway to retrieve his coat.

Petra gave him a faint smile just as a gust of wind blew the front door wide open, almost knocking Dustin into the wall and blowing the ash clean off her cigarette.

'Don't leave it too long,' he said, gesturing to the door. 'It's not just the house that needs some TLC,' he added, throwing on his coat and blowing her a kiss.

With that, he stepped back out into the downpour once more, but just as he was about to close the door behind him, another gust of wind slammed the door shut in his face.

The daisy pendant around Petra's neck radiated a gentle warmth, as if it was content once more.

Petra discarded the extinguished cigarette and turned her attention back to Nathan, who suddenly seemed like he had seen a ghost as he stood there shaking, looking as white as a sheet, still holding the photo frame and talking to himself.

'Well I don't like him, Will, and I don't like you either, you're mean and horrible to me,' Nathan said, quivering.

Petra approached him and knelt down to give him a hug and removed the photo from his hands, tears welling up again.

'Oh, Nathan, my poor son,' Petra said, pulling him in tighter. 'I thought those days of your imaginary friend being around had long since gone.'

'Guess again, bitch!' Nathan screamed through a

deeper pitch than his own normal voice, as he struggled out of her grasp.

Petra, taken aback and in shock, slapped his face. 'Don't you dare talk to Mummy like that!' she roared.

Then all of a sudden, the glass in the frame shattered into a thousand pieces, exploding over their heads. Petra reasoned the stress and tightness she held it had caused it to shatter. She screamed out loud in surprise as Nathan then suddenly turned menacingly to her. 'Tough luck. Nathan's not here right now. I am and I'm getting stronger all the time, I am going to get what I want and no one will challenge me, especially him,' he said, pointing to Stan in the photo of the now glassless frame.

The pendant beat hard against Petra's chest and gave her an inner strength she didn't know she had. Petra threw her arms around Nathan and brought him close, into a warm embrace.

A mother's love and the unseen force of the pendant connected with the dark soul that was within Nathan, making the child scream out as if in pain, before he collapsed, defeated in her arms. 'I'm sorry Mummy, I won't let him hurt you again,' he said, sobbing, whilst burrowing his head into hers.

Later that night, having tucked a miserable Nathan into his bed, Petra returned downstairs and fixed herself a stiff drink. It was a dusty bottle of half-drunk whiskey that had belonged to Stan, from a long time ago.

As she stood over the bin cradling the glass of whiskey, Petra looked at the remnants of the broken glass and frame with sadness in her eyes.

She gulped down a large shot and retrieved the

now crumpled photo from her jeans pocket, to look longingly at the image of loving memories from long ago.

'Why did you have to leave me, Stan?' she whispered, but she knew no answer would come.

She made her way to the back door that overlooked a messy garden, overgrown with wild flowers intermingled with weeds, as she gazed up into the night sky.

She knew Nathan was unlike any other child of his age. He often spoke of his other mummy and of some past life that Petra could not understand, but she had never got round to taking him to a physician.

It was like Nathan harboured an ancient soul that had gotten itself attached to her son.

The imaginary friend of his had now manifested again, but this time it was more malevolent than previous past encounters. As Nathan got older, so the other persona got stronger.

It called itself Will. Could it be the same Will that sacrificed himself to save Stan from the minibus wreckage all those years ago? Was it just a coincidence? Had she imagined Nathan saying the name? Or was it a name he heard in passing?

Petra thought long and hard, but in the end she finished her drink and decided to put it down to the overactive imagination of a sensitive son, who had no father to idolise, even though he was still too young to fully understand.

Petra popped her empty glass into the cluttered sink, strode over to the wooden urn, gave it a gentle kiss and retired to bed.

She hoped Nathan would outgrow this difficult

time and mature into a wonderful man one day, just like his dad Stanley had been.

Another long night lay ahead, with a large, cold bed waiting, the only warmth from the pit of her stomach slowly draining away as the whisky subsided.

RESURRECTOR

Making sure his sister Anastasia and her husband were sound asleep, Nathan Palmer, now 16 years old, gently closed their bedroom door and hoisted the satchel over his shoulder, containing three fireworks, loaded with a teaspoon of his father's ashes sealed in each of them, prepped and ready for tomorrow's launch with his family. But he had other ideas.

Most of his father's ashes had been buried already and were now marked by a moderate headstone up in the old cemetery. He was not aware of the traces of his late dad's ashes that were infused with his mum's daisy glass pendant that she wore around her neck.

His sister, for the last couple of years had been kind enough to put him up in a spare room that was originally going to be a nursery, but she and her husband were never able to conceive. They felt great love towards Nathan even though he was a nightmare to live with. But they would never see him out on the street, so were happy to convert it into his lodgings.

The wayward young Nathan was forever getting in to some kind of trouble or other and in the end his stepfather had intervened against Petra's wishes and finally kicked him out of the family home.

Nathan was thankful for his sister accommodating him.

Creeping downstairs, Nathan eyed the car keys sitting in the drop-off point on the hallway dresser and slipped them into his pocket, before stealing out into the darkness of the bleak, wet and miserable night.

He approached the dark blue sedan, clicked the door to unlock on the fob and opened the door.

Twenty minutes later, he had picked up two of his equally troubled friends and was now recklessly steering the stolen vehicle down the puddle-strewn streets, avoiding the sparse traffic as he veered in and out of any cars that crossed his path.

Turning up the bass on the volume of the in-car stereo, Nathan narrowly avoided bouncing up a kerb and wiping out a middle-aged couple, huddled under a brightly coloured golfing umbrella, as they walked silently hand in hand along a desolate pavement.

Nathan looked into the vibrating rear-view mirror to his friend Cade, who was swigging from a can of beer in the back seat. 'Cade, pull down the back and look for anything interesting in the boot?'

'Okay, sure. What am I looking for?' Cade said, tossing the now empty can out of the window.

'I don't know, anything useful,' Nathan said, as a headlight from a trailing car lit up his darkened wicked eyes in the mirror.

'Haiden, pass me a beer and roll me a snout,' Nathan said, presenting the passenger to his left a tobacco tin from his black bomber jacket pocket.

'Lots of crap back here,' Cade shouted over his shoulder, squirming around half buried in the boot, flashing the light from his mobile phone around its darkened interior.

Increasing the speed and hurtling around a bend into a black mirrored puddle, Nathan smirked, as the car aquaplaned through, showering a homeless man hunkered down for the night in a shop porch.

'Well let's see what we've got then,' he said.

Cade returned from the black void wielding a pair of old wellingtons and a set of jump leads. 'Like I said, nothing of interest... Wait a minute though, what's this down in the foot well?' he said, discarding the items in hand.

Reaching down, he pulled on a long-handled tool and grunted as he pulled it up onto his lap to study it. 'Got ourselves a sledgehammer, is this useful enough?' he beamed.

Nathan grinded the gears as he shifted up. 'Yeah, I was hoping that was still in here, noticed it a few days ago. Might come in handy, Cade. Haiden, you rolled that cigarette yet?'

Haiden had just finished running the paper's glue across his tongue. 'Hmm, here you go,' he said, rolling it closed and running his fingers around it to seal it up properly.

Nathan snatched it from his hands and stuck it behind his ear. 'Light?'

Haiden fished a lighter from his jeans pocket and passed it along with the tobacco tin to Nathan. 'So where we going anyway?' he said, proceeding to reach down to retrieve a cold can of beer from between his feet.

'I think we should smash up some bus stops or parked cars,' Cade said, wielding the sledgehammer over his shoulder and pretending to bring it down onto Haiden's head.

Haiden grabbed a hold of the heavy steel end. 'Leave it out, Cade, you idiot, I'm not getting in to trouble again with you,' he said, trying to wrestle the hammer from Cade's grasp.

'Don't worry, I've got something better to do with that,' Nathan said, taking the sledgehammer off both of them and laying it across his lap.

Eventually the blue sedan with the louts sped past the main road containing a row of various shops and travel agents, and they made their way to a church sitting grand on a crest of a hill.

They were now driving on the wrong side of the road and swerved at the last minute to avoid an oncoming van containing two undertakers that were on a coroner's call-out.

Nathan, with only malice on his mind, didn't even recognise one of the occupants of the vehicle they just missed as being Dustin, who had definitely recognised his stepson driving his sister-in-law's stolen car.

'Seriously! He will be the death of me,' Dustin said, hitting the brakes, sending the wheeled trolley in the van's rear hold slamming into the dividing steel wall behind their seats.

'Too bloody right,' the passenger, Blake, said, leaning out of his window into the downpour of the night. 'See you real soon, morons!' he shouted after them.

'Oh, we will see them before they see us,' Dustin said, slamming the van into a three-point turn.

'You what? What are you doing, Dusty?' Blake said, reeling his head back in from the sleet that battered his face.

'Going after them. That boy who was driving the car... that's my stepson Nate. When I catch up with him, I'll throttle him,' Dustin said, forcing the steering wheel hard right and lurching the van forward, kicking up loose gravel between its tyre treads.

'What about our callout? We've got less than thirty minutes now to get to the scene to collect our deceased. We can't risk losing the contract. I for one don't want to lose my job over it,' Blake exclaimed, checking his seatbelt was still securely fastened.

'Screw it, I'm not letting this one slide. Nate has put my wife Petra through enough over the years as it is,' Dustin replied.

Fast approaching the green traffic lights that were up ahead, Dustin noticed the lads' car disappearing down the lane that split between the church and the vicarage.

The neon green reflection of the light, rippled across the surface of the oily puddle as the van's wheels cut through its wake.

'You're well over the speed limit, Dusty, the tracker is going to flag this up in the morning. Slow down, will you? I don't want to end up in a wagon like this one just yet,' Blake said, anxiously gripping both his knees hard, as they passed through the lights.

Dustin didn't hear him, he was too focused on catching up with the lead vehicle and had misjudged the corner of the narrow lane, as a rogue branch collided with the wing mirror and yanked it clean off.

'Whoa! Now we're going to have to pay for the damage too,' Blake cried, wishing he had been given a different on-call partner.

'Just shut up, Blake!' Dustin said, with anger boiling over.

By the time the removal vehicle had caught up to

the sedan, the occupants had long abandoned it and were well on their way, picking a path through the church cemetery.

Nathan was dragging the sledgehammer behind him with his satchel around his neck, the fireworks jostled around the hold as they poked out from beneath the flap. Haiden and Cade were vaulting over headstones to catch him up.

'We're not going to smash the church up, are we?' Haiden asked nervously.

'No! I'm going to find my dad, the man who ruined my life,' Nathan said, rounding the corner of the church.

Cade shouted after him, 'I thought he was... you know... dead?' he said, in hushed tones.

'He is. But a voice inside, is telling me I've got to see him. I can't explain it though, so just go with it, alright?' Nathan said, sounding impatient as he found the grave's marker and came to an abrupt halt.

Nathan's friends exchanged troubled looks. 'He's not thinking of digging up his dad, is he?' Haiden said, on the quiet to Cade.

'I bloody well hope not,' Haiden hissed.

'What's more worrying is the voice inside his head that he complains about all the time. I hope he's not schitzo,' Haiden added, starting to freak out with the eerie silence that had now descended upon them.

Gathering around the weathered headstone, Haiden and Cade eyed Nathan cautiously, as they slowed down upon catching him up.

'So, err, what are we going to do now?' Cade said, yanking a full can of beer from his oversized pockets to drink from, for Dutch courage.

Not getting an immediate answer, Cade pulled off the can's ring pull and slurped from it, fearful of the answer that he was sure to hear, that he knew would eventually come.

Nathan pulled the rolled-up cigarette from his ear and lit it up. 'Now. I'll tell you what now. I'm going to obliterate this headstone,' he said, taking a slow burning puff.

He took another few pulls on the cigarette and removed the satchel from his shoulder, casually dumping it on the floor. 'Grab a firework each from the bag and both of you split up. Haiden, go stand over there,' he said, pointing to a nearby tree. 'Cade, you over there,' he added, pointing to a grave thirty yards to the left of Haiden. 'I'm going to put the last one in the ground just behind my dad's headstone, pointing directly at it. I want a triangle formation and I want them all pointed at my dad's headstone... GOT IT!' he demanded, taking his firework from the satchel and walking around to the rear of the black, marble headstone.

Cade and Haiden dutifully nodded, grabbed a firework obediently, then went to take up positions.

Once all fireworks were in position, Nathan walked back round to the front of the headstone and swung the hammer up over his shoulder, and poised himself, ready to strike down into it, with brute force.

'Once I've smashed this and gone to light my firework, then I want you both to set off yours... no matter what happens, understand?' he huffed, with the cigarette hanging from his lips.

Cade and Haiden nodded.

'I suggest you light them at the same time I do

mine, you got it?' Nathan said, looking to each of them in turn with a wild rage in his eyes.

The friends nodded again, then gave each other a puzzled look.

Nathan's hands felt cold and clammy as he gripped hard onto the sledgehammer. The rain flattened his blond spiky hair, causing the gel to run down his forehead.

With an almighty swing, the hammer hit the headstone and cleaved it in two, just as a fork of lightning cracked the dark clouded sky, blotting out the noise of the impact.

Nathan fell to his knees and dropped the hammer beside him. 'Dad! Show yourself,' he said, fighting back the tears, then added, 'William Last wants a word with you.'

Unseen to his friends, a mist began to ooze from the jagged remains of the split headstone, slowly swirling and taking shape into the form of a man... Nathan's dad... Stanley Palmer.

It was just at that instance when Dustin came storming into view with a fiery temper, from around the corner of the church, having left his partner inspecting the van's damage.

'Nate. What the hell do you think you're...?' Dustin trailed off, seeing what Nathan had done. 'My god, boy, are you really that sick?' he said, grabbing Nathan from behind by both shoulders and hauling him to his feet.

Nathan spun around uncontrollably, lunged for the sledgehammer and swung it hard into Dustin's shoulder, which made a large cracking sound as it splintered bone, shattering his stepfather's scapula.

Dustin fell, screaming in agony to the wet, mud-stricken ground.

'Your little Nate is no more, Dusty. I, William Last, am here now and all shall answer to me,' the deep growl of Will bellowed.

The ghostly memory of Stanley Palmer, having now fully developed into a clearer image from the eerie mist, floated across to the now-possessed Nathan.

'Will, you don't have to do this, please release my son before it's too late. You can both come through this unscathed. One way or another you cannot continue on this dark path,' the spectral image said, with an air of calm and grace.

Haiden and Cade, now in horror after seeing the pain inflicted on Nathan's stepdad, awkwardly glanced at one another, lit the fireworks laden with Stan's ashes and ran off, petrified, into the night.

William Last, now in control of Nathan's form, howled into the storm as he realised the fireworks were lit too soon. 'No! I'm not ready yet,' he screamed, slipping and sliding as he raced over to light his own firework.

Dustin pulled himself up, cradling his arm, and approached the ghost of Stan, that he now saw before him. Disbelievingly and in shock, he pleaded, 'Stan. Stanley, is that really you? I, I'm sorry, I'm so sorry for killing Heparin, your beloved cat... Please forgive me,' he said, crying loudly with pain and regret.

But they were to be the last words that came out of his mouth.

The lit fireworks had burnt away the fuse and ignited the gunpowder, shooting across the cemetery in a hot fiery haze, hitting him with double force, in an explosion of bangs and whizzes.

Dustin's screams penetrated the silent night, as he then went running blindly through the cemetery in flames, billowing smoke behind him with the rain sizzling off his burning body.

Will went to turn back when he realised what happened. The plan was to shoot the ashes of Stan at Stan's own ghost, which in turn would break Stan's astral link to this world.

Then he, Will, could go unchecked and create an army on Earth with no Stan from beyond the grave to stop him.

Sensing Will's intention of reaching the last remaining firework for reasons he did not yet comprehend, and still feeling great sadness for Dustin's demise behind him, which smouldered in the night, for in the afterlife he had learned to forgive all injustices, Stan summoned with all his energy a calling of five angels to show themselves at his bequest.

Sure enough and to Will's disgust, moments later, five spectral winged angels materialised in a circle around him.

Will lit the last firework with wet, shaking hands from the hot-embered tip of his cigarette, swung the firework round and pointed it at the ghost of Stan.

The angels were too slow to close rank and their feeble efforts to protect Stan by sacrificing themselves, were in vain as the rocket found its mark.

Stanley Palmer did not know the true intent of the firework's purpose and that it could erase his one shot of stopping Will's world domination.

The ark of light with the holy, ashen remains of Stan exploded in a carousel of dancing colour, sending Stan's surprised spirit back once more, to the astral plane from where he came.

William Last flashed a wicked grin to the advancing angels that had him now surrounded in a circle. 'You've no way of getting home now, little birds, and your power has no anchor here without Stan. I'm going to enjoy converting you to my cause. But first, I don't like the white of your feathers so I think I'm going to make them blood red as I clip them,' he said, bringing his hands up and uprooting all the headstones in the cemetery with an unseen telekinetic force, that sent large clods of earth flying outwards around him.

A light came on from a window in the vicarage nearby, just as the angels looked around nervously at a darker cloud descending over them. A swirling torrent of heavy-set headstones circled overhead.

It was if a tornado had uprooted them and was now pulling them up, spinning into the heart of its funnel.

Yanking back the curtains, a chubby vicar peered out from the confines of his domain. What he saw unfolding before him, was the work of the devil.

The letters 'R.I.P.' engraved within some of the headstones now held greater meaning, as they targeted their prey from high above, before raining down with fire and brimstone with lethal force on the winged victims below.

The vicar's heart gave out. He clutched at his chest and fell away from the frame of the window.

Nathan Palmer's soul was now truly lost, as William's evil spirit took hold of his diminishing light entirely.

William Last had finally acquired power on Earth to wield an unimaginable, supernatural power.

Dustin, lay motionless and quite dead, smoking in the ruined grounds of the cemetery.

Stanley Palmer was banished back to the afterlife with very few options left to prevent any further catastrophes happening on Earth as he was tasked to do.

Petra Palmer, asleep in her lonely bed, held the softly humming pendant close to her chest, now a widow once more.

Any glimmer of faith and hope was fading fast, as the tulpa, William Last, an evil figment, made flesh of Stan's once troubled mind, was resurrected to stake his claim on Earth.

For the outside world, it was as if a remote, freak hurricane was taking place.

The trapped Nathan Palmer, now a slave to his split personality, thought he was having a schizophrenic episode, as his alter ego laughed menacingly into the night.

The first book of the Oasis trilogy, THE OASIS OF HOPE by Matthew Newell is available on Amazon.

Printed in Great Britain
by Amazon